"You should have let me do that," she said on seeing the coffee was well underway.

"It's all right, Ruby," Sebastian replied, trying to make up in some small way for his earlier abruptness. "I can make my own coffee."

"But it's my job, Mr. Marshall," she protested. "Here. You go and relax somewhere and I'll bring the coffee to you. I know how you like it," she added with a smile that was as sweet and as perversely sexy as she was.

When she came right up to where he was standing by the coffee machine, he caught a whiff of something tantalizing. The scent wafting from her person was a mixture of coconut and vanilla. Not perfume as such. Possibly shampoo. Without thinking, he leaned closer and inhaled, his nose not far from her hair.

Delicious, he thought once again. Everything about her was delicious. Delicious and dangerous and disturbingly tempting!

Gritting his teeth, he whirled around and strode away before he did or said anything seriously stupid. Ruby was, after all, his housekeeper. Which meant she was strictly off-limits.

So why was it that this thought didn't help dampen what was going on inside him? If anything, her being forbidden fruit made everything harder.

A note from the editor

Dear Reader,

For decades Miranda Lee has delighted readers around the globe with her spellbinding love stories, and her books have been an entry point for many readers and authors alike into the wonderful world of Harlequin romances. Now it's my honor to present to you this very special romance, *The Billionaire's Cinderella Housekeeper*, which marks Miranda's retirement from Harlequin Presents.

In this, her Harlequin Presents swan song, Miranda brings you the compelling romance between sensible housekeeper Ruby and brooding billionaire Sebastian. In the close quarters of Sebastian's Sydney mansion, sparks fly between the unlikely couple and ignite a powerful passion neither can resist! But with their hearts still bruised from past hurts, will they ever give in to more than lust?

I hope you enjoy finding out in Ruby and Sebastian's story! And with over ninety books to her name, Miranda has an incredible legacy of alpha heroes, fiery heroines and stunning Australian settings that you can continue to enjoy from Harlequin.com.

All that's left to say is a heartfelt congratulations to Miranda on an amazing writing career with Harlequin that will endure long after readers have turned the last page on this story...

Happy reading!

Carly Byrne

Editor

Miranda Lee

THE BILLIONAIRE'S CINDERELLA HOUSEKEEPER

HARLEQUIN®
PRESENTS®

Recycling programs for this product may not exist in your area.

ISBN-13: 978-1-335-40392-6

The Billionaire's Cinderella Housekeeper

Copyright © 2021 by Miranda Lee

For questions and comments about the quality of this book, please contact us at CustomerService@Harlequin.com.

Harlequin Enterprises ULC
22 Adelaide St. West, 40th Floor
Toronto, Ontario M5H 4E3, Canada
www.Harlequin.com

Printed in U.S.A.

Born and raised in the Australian bush, **Miranda Lee** was boarding school educated, and briefly pursued a career in classical music before moving to Sydney and embracing the world of computers. Happily married with three daughters, she began writing when family commitments kept her at home. She likes to create stories that are believable, modern, fast-paced and sexy. Her interests include meaty sagas, doing word puzzles, gambling and going to the movies.

Dedicated to all my loyal readers over the years.

Thank you from the bottom of my heart.

Love from Miranda Lee

CHAPTER ONE

'So, you're looking for a live-in housekeeping position, are you, Ruby?' the lady asked.

Ruby heard the scepticism behind the woman's words. She'd heard it before from the other employment agencies she'd been to. They'd all taken one look at her, along with her less than impressive résumé, and told her they didn't have anything suitable on their books right now.

'Yes, that's right,' she replied, already knowing she'd drawn a blank again.

Ruby suppressed a sigh. If she couldn't get a live-in position, then she'd have to take Oliver up on his offer for her to stay on at his place. Liam had offered to have her too, but really, she didn't want to live with either of her brothers. Neither of their apartments were what you would call spacious. Besides, Oliver's long-time girlfriend, Rachel, lived with him, and Liam's new girlfriend, Lara, had just moved in with him. They needed their own space, as did she.

'You do realise,' the woman said kindly, 'that Housewives For Hire doesn't often have such a position available. We specialise more in part-time casual housekeeping. Rarely live-in. Most of my girls are married women who want to earn money whilst their children are at school.'

'I see,' Ruby said in a flat voice. Obviously, it had been a mistake to come back to Sydney and try to embrace real life again.

But before Ruby could say goodbye and go, a phone buzzed on the desk and Barbara, the owner of Housewives for Hire, swept it up, mouthing an apology to Ruby as she did so.

Ruby didn't really listen as the conversation was rather one-sided. Barbara just said *yes* and *hmm* a lot whilst tapping on her computer, so Ruby tuned out, putting her mind to the problem of what she would do now, because blind Freddie could see she wasn't going to get a housekeeping job in Sydney. She'd been a fool to think it would be straightforward to get such a position.

Going back to her nomadic lifestyle, however, no longer appealed. It had served its purpose for the past five years, giving her the time out she'd desperately needed. But when she'd turned thirty on her last birthday, a yearning had started growing inside her, a yearning to settle down and do something worthwhile with her life.

Not marriage. Lord no. Ruby shuddered at the thought. After the fiasco with Jason a few years back, she'd decided that marriage would never be her lot in life. Because marriage meant loving and trusting a man with her happiness, and Ruby simply couldn't see that happening.

And let's face it, Ruby thought, *Jason wasn't the*

only member of the opposite sex to have a strike against him. Your father sowed the seeds for your distrust when you were only nineteen, with your first serious boyfriend, Bailey, compounding your negative feelings shortly after.

It was inevitable that she would eventually come to the decision to rely on herself, and herself alone. Jason had just been the catalyst that had propelled her into adopting a totally celibate lifestyle, which Ruby found she actually quite liked. She enjoyed the freedom from the emotional complications associated with boyfriends and sex.

To her surprise, she found she didn't miss either. Not one little bit.

The idea had finally taken hold that she could become a social worker. Over the past few years of travelling and working all over Queensland and northern NSW, she'd come across a lot of unfortunates who could have had different lives if someone had given them a helping hand.

The only problem with this was that social workers these days had degrees.

Gradually, Ruby had come up with a plan. It had seemed so simple on paper. She would return to Sydney and get herself a live-in housekeeping position, not because she really wanted to be a housekeeper but because that way she wouldn't have to pay rent. Rents in Sydney, she knew, were exorbitant, and she didn't have enough savings to pay a bond, plus the first month's rent in advance. On top of that, she could spend her spare time doing an online course to get herself into a university so that she could study for a social science degree.

In her head, by thirty-five she would be a qualified social worker. Ruby knew she was intelligent and if she put her mind to it, she could do just about anything.

Unfortunately, her plan seemed to have one fatal flaw. No one would hire her as a housekeeper, not even here in Sydney where there were loads of such positions advertised. Ruby suspected her lack of experience in such a position was the main reason for her always being turned down, although one of the agencies had hinted that she looked too…sexy.

Now that had really floored her, though, now she thought about it, she had come across this opinion once or twice before over recent years. Lord knew why. Okay, so she had what was considered a good figure nowadays but she wasn't even pretty.

Ruby shook her head ruefully when she thought back to her teenage years. No one would have called her sexy back then. Lord no! The opposite sex hadn't given her a second glance when she was at school. And why would they? She'd been all puppy fat and braces, along with the lack of confidence that went with puberty. It had taken every bit of courage she possessed to apply for a job at a local fast-food place. But from then on her confidence had grown, confidence that had nothing to do with looks. It annoyed her that people couldn't see past the obvious to who she was inside.

Oh, well. Ruby accepted she would *have* to live with one of her brothers for a while till she could get a job as a waitress or bar staff—jobs she was well qualified for and where looking sexy would be an asset. Once she had enough money she would look for shared accommodation, hopefully with a room of her own so she could study in peace.

It wouldn't be as good as her original plan of being a live-in housekeeper but it would have to do, Ruby decided as she waited for Barbara to finish her call. A potential client, it sounded like.

'I see,' Barbara said slowly. 'So this won't be a permanent position, Mr Marshall. Your usual housekeeper will be coming back to work for you eventually.'

Ruby couldn't hear what Mr Marshall said to this.

'Actually,' Barbara went on with a glance Ruby's way, 'I do have a girl who might suit you very well. Yes, she has excellent references.'

Ruby nodded enthusiastically at this. She did have excellent references. Ruby was a good worker, and as honest as the day was long. Employers were always sorry to see her go.

'She's actually here now. Would you like to talk to her? Good. Her name's Ruby. Here she is.'

The ball's in your court, Barbara's eyes seemed to say as she handed Ruby the phone.

'Hello?' Ruby said after a swift swallow. She was not a nervous person, but she did so want this job. Even if it was only temporary. Because then she would have *experience* as a housekeeper on her résumé, which would lead more easily to getting another housekeeping position.

'Hi, Ruby,' Mr Marshall said in a deep and very masculine voice, the kind of voice you mostly associated with radio announcers and soul singers. 'First things first. Have you done housekeeping jobs before?'

Ruby was about to say no when she had a light-bulb moment. Really, why hadn't she thought to mention this before?

'Not professionally,' she said briskly. 'But I ran the family household for seven years from the age of eighteen till I was twenty-five. My mother was ill at the time,' she raced on before he could ask why. She didn't add that her mother had actually died of ovarian cancer a year after she'd finished school, her precious father leaving it up to Ruby to help her shattered younger brothers through school and then university. The rotten mongrel deserted them two months after the funeral to live with his rich mistress in her fancy city penthouse. Yes, he'd given them the family house to live in and, yes, he'd paid the bills, but that had been the extent of his support.

'I did all the cooking and cleaning,' she added, in case Mr Marshall thought they'd been rich enough to pay someone to do that.

'Your mother must have been very proud of you,' he remarked. 'And is she well now?'

Ruby blanked from her mind the grief that still consumed her whenever she thought of her lovely, brave mother. 'No,' she bit out, gritting her teeth at the same time. 'She passed away. Cancer.'

'Bloody cancer,' Mr Marshall muttered, then was silent for a few seconds. 'Sorry,' he said at last. 'My wife died of cancer. Still, no use going on about it, is there?' he continued gruffly before she could make any sympathetic noises. 'Only makes things worse. What's done is done. So, how old are you now, Ruby?'

'Thirty.'

'I see. And what have you been doing with yourself since your mother's death?'

Clearly, he thought her mother had died fairly recently and not a decade earlier. Ruby decided not to enlighten him as it would only mean answering awkward questions that weren't really relevant to this interview. She hated talking about that time in her life. *Hated* it!

'Well, I've always worked part-time in the hospitality industry,' she explained, 'even when I was at school. So once I had the opportunity I took off by myself, travelling all over northern NSW and Queensland, working in various resorts and clubs. I've done lots of things, from serving behind the bar to waitressing to the occasional bit of work as a receptionist. But I'm a little tired of that life, so I've come back to Sydney to find suitable work whilst I study for a degree in social science.'

'That sounds very commendable. And you sound like a very nice girl. Not that Housewives For Hire ever recommends any other kind. I have it on good authority that they're very reputable, so I'm sure you'll be fine for the job. Unfortunately, I'm in London on business at the moment and I won't be back in Sydney for over a week. I hate leaving my house empty so this is what I'll do. My sister lives in Sydney in a nearby suburb—I live in Mosman—and she has keys to my house. I'll contact her and have her meet with you there tomorrow morning. She can show you the house and answer any questions you might have about me. But if you want it, then the job's yours, Ruby.'

If she wanted it? Of course she wanted it. Wanted it like crazy! He sounded like such a nice man. 'Oh,

Mr Marshall, that's wonderful. I'll do a good job. I promise.'

'I'm sure you will. Now hand the phone back to Barbara for me so I can give her my sister's details. Yes, yes,' he said impatiently to someone in the background. 'I won't be long. You go down to breakfast and I'll join you there.'

Ruby handed the phone back and just sat there, dazed and elated, whilst Barbara spoke to Mr Marshall and tapped some more on her computer. Finally, the woman hung up and turned her swivel chair to face her.

'You're a lucky girl, Ruby,' she said with a smile on her face. 'Mr Marshall is none other than Sebastian Marshall, head of Harvest Productions, which you may or may not have heard of.'

She hadn't, and shook her head in the negative.

'They produce several highly successful television shows,' Barbara went on. 'I'm sure you'd have heard of them. *Australia at Noon*… *What Word Am I*? The soapie *Elizabeth Street*. But the jewel in their crown is *Battle at the Bar*.'

'That's a very popular show,' Ruby agreed, despite only having watched it the once. But she'd heard a lot about it and was always meaning to watch the series some more. The hero, or anti-hero really, was a lawyer named Caesar Battle who defended the sometimes indefensible and often won. A loner, he was an enigmatic character who worked hard and played hard but still had an integrity about him that was very likeable. Women lusted after him. Men wanted to be him. The show had won countless awards, especially for its handsome main actor whose name eluded her.

'I'm sorry it's only a temporary position,' Barbara continued, 'but it's better than nothing.'

'*Much* better,' Ruby agreed with a smile.

'The job won't be too hard, either. Mr Marshall is a widower, with no children.'

'So how old is Mr Marshall?' It had been impossible to tell from his voice. A widower, however, suggested someone elderly.

'Forty, according to the internet,' came the crisp reply.

'Goodness. That young.' Ruby suddenly thought of her father, who'd been forty when he began having an affair. A dangerous age, forty. Or so she'd been told.

Thinking of her father always made Ruby angry. Angry and cynical and just a little wary, when it came to her dealings with men. The last thing she wanted was to stuff up this job by presenting herself with the wrong look.

'Does your company have a dress code?' she asked. 'A uniform perhaps?'

'No. My girls wear whatever they like. Though under your circumstances,' Barbara added with a knowing glint in her eye, 'I would suggest dressing conservatively. Professional.'

Ruby glanced down at her outfit, which she considered reasonably conservative. Yes, the skirt ended above her knee and the top did show a hint of cleavage but by modern standards it was hardly provocative. Still…

'That's very good advice,' she said. 'Thank you.'

'Sensible girl,' Barbara praised. 'Now, I'll just contact Mr Marshall's sister and we'll make arrangements for tomorrow.'

CHAPTER TWO

RUBY WAS EARLY. Partly because she didn't want to risk being late, but mostly because she wanted to have a good look at the house—and the area—all by herself.

She'd expected her new boss's house to be posh. Wealthy people who lived in Mosman didn't live in ordinary houses. And she wasn't disappointed. It *was* posh. So posh and so elegant, in fact, that it took her breath away.

'Oh, my…' She sighed as she climbed out of her car and just stared.

The house was white, cement-rendered and two-storeyed, with an architectural style that reminded Ruby of those old Georgian mansions that were popular with the English aristocracy.

Not that this house was on that scale, but it had a size and symmetry that were very pleasing to the eye, with a central ivy-clad portico flanked by two French doors downstairs and the same number of windows upstairs. The front yard was like a miniature Versailles garden, with manicured hedges and gravel areas rather than lawn, highlighted with exquisite pots and water features. The front fence had a solid white concrete base topped with dark wooden slats, and a wooden security gate that opened onto a wide path made of white marble tiles. Not that Ruby could open the gate, but there were gaps you could see through.

For a few moments Ruby wondered if she'd bitten off more than she could chew. But then common sense kicked in. Of course she could do this. She was a very resourceful person. And what was the worst that could happen? She stuffed it up and got fired. Not the end of the world.

Ruby refused to succumb to what her mother used to call the heebie-jeebies.

Ruby smiled at the memory. Her mother had been such a character, a great reader who loved cute sayings such as heebie-jeebies. Being a nervous Nellie was another of her favourites, perhaps because her mother had been an anxious person growing up. She'd confided once that she'd been determined to raise Ruby to be confident and independent in her thinking.

Ruby believed she had eventually achieved this, though only after many life lessons.

A car coming slowly up the street brought Ruby's mind back to the present. When she saw a woman behind the wheel of the Lexus she just knew it was Mr Marshall's sister.

The Lexus pulled in behind her silver Kia Rio, which, whilst not a flash car, was still fairly new and sparkling clean, Ruby having left it at a car wash whilst she shopped last night. She knew how important first impressions were and was glad Barbara had advised her how not to dress. Because Ruby was no fool. She knew that if Mr Marshall's sister didn't like the look of her, she might not be getting this job.

Ruby was pleased with the way the woman was smiling at her. Clearly, the outfit she'd bought last night was spot on. The A-line black skirt reached her knees, and the simple white shirt she'd teamed with it shouted professionalism, especially when combined with black pumps and pulled-back hair.

'Ruby, I presume?' the woman said as she approached. She was slim and blonde and rather glamorous-looking. In her forties, Ruby guessed, but could have been older. Money did keep women looking young, what with Botox and face peels.

'Yes,' Ruby replied. 'And you must be Mrs Chalmers.'

'Indeed, but do call me Gloria,' she insisted, her blue eyes twinkling with genuine warmth.

Ruby could not help liking her. But then, Ruby liked most people, as long as they were nice to her.

'That's a lovely name,' she said.

'A little old-fashioned. I much prefer Ruby. So, Ruby, what do you think of my brother's house?'

'It's very impressive.'

'It is. I have the keys here. Shall we go inside?'

'Yes, please.'

The inside was as elegant as the facade, with lots of grey marble floors and white walls, and a mixture of pale silk curtains and plantation shutters at the windows. Some of the furniture looked antique, in dark wood, but the overall impression was very contemporary. The kitchen was a dream in mostly white, with every mod con imaginable, including a coffee machine, which Ruby would have no trouble using. There were several reception rooms, and one carpeted bedroom downstairs, which she imagined a housekeeper might use, with a bathroom just across the hallway. Upstairs there were three guest double bedrooms—again carpeted—serviced by a family bathroom, along with a huge master suite, which had its own sitting area, bathroom and walk-in wardrobe.

Though not quite a mansion, it was still going to take some looking after. Maybe she wouldn't have much time to study after all.

'You look a little worried,' Gloria said as she led Ruby through some French doors out onto the huge back terrace, which was set up for alfresco dining. Beyond the terrace was a large lawned backyard along with a rectangular swimming pool to one side.

'Will I have any help?' she asked.

'Goodness yes. There's a cleaner who comes in Monday and Friday to do the floors and the bathrooms. Her name is Janice. Though she wouldn't have come today with Sebastian being away. Then there's a handyman called Tom who does the garden and the pool. Not sure which days he's here, but Georgia will tell you everything.'

'Georgia?'

'Sebastian's usual housekeeper. She's left you the house phone with all the necessary contacts in it, including her own phone number. It's in the drawer in the kitchen just below the cutlery drawer. She wants you to ring her today so she can fill you in on everything Sebastian likes and doesn't like.'

'Right. So what happened that she had to be called away so suddenly?'

'Didn't Sebastian tell you?'

'No.'

'Typical,' Gloria said, rolling her eyes. 'Her sister had a car accident and will be in hospital for several weeks.'

'Oh, the poor love. So where did this happen? Obviously not here in Sydney.'

'No, down in Melbourne. Georgia said she will most likely stay for a good while, even after her sister gets out of hospital. There are three children to look after and her brother-in-law is pretty useless, she said. Anyway, she won't be back for at least three months.'

'Barbara said it might be as long as that.'

'Barbara?' Gloria frowned.

'The woman who runs Housewives for Hire.'

'Oh, right. Look, I'm sorry to love you and leave you but I have some ladies coming over for lunch today and I've still got a lot to do. Here are the keys. Make yourself at home, and please do ring me if you have any questions, though I imagine Georgia would be better qualified to answer them than me. Oh, and one last thing, there's a side driveway which leads down to a huge garage underneath the house. There's plenty of room for your car. Do use it. The remote is on the key ring. Also, Sebastian said to tell you he'll be in contact. Probably by text. Or email. Now, I have to run. Lovely meeting you, Ruby. Give my regards to Georgia when you ring her. Bye.'

She was gone before Ruby could do more than say bye in return, leaving Ruby standing there on the back terrace, still slightly overawed by the place. She'd worked in some fancy resorts but she'd never been in a private home this flash before. Her own family home—which her father had sold once they'd all flown the nest—had been a standard brick veneer house in the Western suburbs with three bedrooms, one and a half bathrooms and no pool. Even so, it had sold for over a million dollars. Lord knew what this place was worth. Or what Sebastian Marshall was worth, for that matter.

Her curiosity piqued, Ruby decided to do an internet search on him after she'd parked her car and settled in. Hopefully, there would be a photo or two so she could see what he looked like. She'd expected there to be a few photos of him around the house but there weren't. Not a one. Clearly, he wasn't into photos. She wondered why. People usually had a few photos dotted around their home, photos of family and loved ones. At the very least, she'd expected a few photos of him with his wife. But there wasn't a single one. All she could think was that he didn't want to be reminded of his marriage, or his dead wife, which was a shame. She loved looking at all the photos of her mother she had on her phone. She'd even had a tribute to her mother tattooed on her wrist with the dates of her birth and death inside a love heart. When you loved someone, you wanted to remember them.

It was a puzzle all right.

Hopefully Georgia could fill in a few of the blanks when Ruby rang her, plus give her a feel for what sort of man her new boss was. A personal connection was much better than the internet. But first she would make herself some coffee with that lovely coffee machine.

There was nothing better than good coffee, Ruby thought as she walked back inside and headed for the kitchen. Coffee always relaxed her, and she needed relaxing after what had been a somewhat stressful morning. But really, it had worked out surprisingly well. Gloria had seemed to like her and the feelings were mutual. And truly, the house was divine. It would be a pleasure living in it and looking after it. On the surface, it was a dream job.

Of course, her satisfaction with the position ultimately rested on the character of her boss. She hoped he would be as nice as he'd sounded on the phone, and not one of those rich, arrogant men she'd met during her working life. Having a lot of money, she'd found, didn't always bring out the best in the male sex.

Such thoughts reminded her to be careful with her appearance during her time here. *Conservative*, Barbara had advised.

I can do conservative, Ruby reassured herself as she switched on the coffee machine.

Okay, so it wasn't her usual style of dressing but no way was she going to do anything to risk this wonderful job. Which meant hair kept up or at least tied back, minimal make-up and jewellery and a very bland wardrobe.

The clothes she wore today were a good start but she would need more. She could hardly wear this outfit every single day, especially once summer got started. It was already very hot and it was only the first week in December. When she rang Georgia she would ask what *she* usually wore during the summer months. And yes, she would subtly question her about what kind of man Sebastian Marshall was.

Ruby wasn't really worried about him, but forewarned was forearmed.

She wasn't to know that fate would conspire against her, making her first meeting with her new boss very awkward indeed.

CHAPTER THREE

WHEN SEBASTIAN EXITED the terminal the heat came as a shock. After spending a fortnight in Europe's winter his body wasn't used to either heat or humidity. Both enveloped him within seconds, making the wait for a taxi very uncomfortable and irritating.

The trip overseas had spoiled him, he realised, the executives of the various companies who wanted to buy his shows sparing nothing in their efforts to woo his agreement to their terms. He'd been chauffeured around everywhere he went, and wined and dined within an inch of his life—not that it had done them much good. Sebastian knew what his shows were worth—especially *Battle at the Bar*—and he'd driven a hard bargain. He would shortly be many million dollars richer, with more money to come. The royalties would roll in for years.

Not that being super rich interested him all that much. After a certain point, what did it gain you really? There was only so much you could spend before it became obscene. He had a lovely home, an excellent wardrobe and a great car. He didn't need a private jet, a yacht, or a holiday home in the Caribbean.

Of course, it was nice to be able to afford five-star restaurants and first-class airfares, along with the best hotels and resorts in the world. Sebastian couldn't deny that he enjoyed the finer things in life. But then, he'd worked hard to be able to afford them. Damned hard.

Still, he would give every cent he had if only Jennifer...

No, no, don't go there, Sebastian warned himself with gritted teeth.

But he was already there, the emotions he'd felt at the time of her cancer diagnosis coming back to haunt him with a vengeance. Not just grief, but bitterness and anger, and that other awful feeling of helplessness. He'd hated that more than anything: that he hadn't been able to *do* anything to save the woman he loved.

Keep looking forward, he lectured himself sternly. *And working hard.* Work was the only thing that kept the memory demons at bay.

He actually loved running Harvest Productions. It had been his saviour, which was a perverse thing to say when his father had had to die for him to inherit the company. But it was strangely true. Sebastian knew that without the challenge he'd faced when confronted with control of a near-insolvent business a few months after Jennifer's death, he would have fallen by the wayside completely. The realisation that he was *needed*, and that he could actually do something to help all those people faced with the prospect of unemployment, had given him the strength to carry on.

'Where you going, mate?' the taxi driver asked as he scooped up Sebastian's luggage.

Sebastian gave himself a mental shake then stepped

forward to open the passenger door of the taxi. 'Mosman,' he said as he climbed in.

'Where in Mosman?' the driver asked after he slid in behind the wheel.

Sebastian gave his address, only then remembering that he'd better text Ruby and let her know he was on his way home. He'd taken a flight one day earlier than intended, spending the night in Singapore, being feted by another billionaire who wanted a piece of Harvest Productions. It was amazing how success brought investors flocking. He'd been polite with the man but he hadn't liked him at all, turning down his offers and flying out first thing this morning, landing at Mascot at just after three this afternoon. By the time he got home it would be close to four. Even so, Ruby wasn't expecting him till tomorrow morning.

Not that he thought this would be a problem. They'd exchanged a couple of texts during the past week and she seemed an easy-going kind of girl who had everything in hand and wouldn't be upset by his early arrival.

He quickly sent off a text, explaining the situation, confident of getting a reply before long. Girls these days lived on their phones, didn't they?

The taxi driver chatted away as they headed for town. Sebastian didn't mind and asked the chap what he liked to watch on television. He often did that, gathering honest feedback about what the everyday person liked and didn't like. He was pleased to hear the man's disgruntlement with the current wave of reality shows, which matched Sebastian's feelings exactly.

Audiences were getting sick of them and craved more escapist entertainment.

'What do you think of *Battle at the Bar*?' he asked.

'That's one of my favourites,' the man answered as he sped through the harbour tunnel. 'My wife's too. Wouldn't miss an episode for the world. I hope they make another season.'

'I'm sure they will,' Sebastian said a little smugly. They'd already aired four seasons here in Australia and the shooting of the last episode of season five was wrapping up this week. 'Man, it's hot today.' He glanced at the outside temperature on the dashboard. It said thirty-seven.

'They say it's going to be hotter tomorrow.'

'Thank heavens for air conditioning, then.'

'You can say that again.'

Sebastian still hadn't heard back from Ruby, a quick check of his phone showing no messages. His text had gone through but there was no answer. That was odd. He frowned. Maybe he should have contacted her sooner.

The taxi dropped him off with his case, Sebastian giving the man a good tip.

'Thanks, mate,' the driver said, and headed off with a wide smile on his face.

Sebastian unlocked the front gate and wheeled his case along the marble path up to the front door. Once inside, he called out Ruby's name but was greeted by silence. No TV on. No sound at all, except for the air conditioning. It was on downstairs but not upstairs, he soon found out. Sebastian turned it on, throwing his case onto the bed to unpack later when the room was cooler.

It was then that he heard a faint splashing noise coming from outside.

Sebastian moved over to the window, which overlooked the pool, his brain already understanding why Ruby hadn't answered his text. She was in the pool.

And why not? It was blisteringly hot.

Sebastian might have joined her if the woman in the pool hadn't suddenly hauled herself out of the water. For a few seconds, she sat there on the side of the pool, dripping water, before slowly, gracefully, standing up.

Sebastian couldn't help it. He actually groaned, squeezing his eyes shut for a split second before opening them again and just staring.

If ever there was a female body designed to make a man drool, it was Ruby's, especially in that zebra-print bikini she was wearing. Heavens!

It was bad enough when she stood still, but even worse when she began to move, reaching for a nearby towel then lifting a hand to release the clip in her hair. It tumbled down, long black wavy hair, which was in as much abundance as her curves. Watching her walk along the side of the pool, patting herself down with the towel, was an exercise in masochism. Sebastian's male body reacted as most male bodies would, his arousal bringing a surge of dismay.

Sebastian couldn't think of anything worse than having a housekeeper who looked like Ruby. His home was more than his castle. It was his refuge, the only place he could totally relax. How could he relax with *that* sashaying around his house?

Quite attractive was how Gloria had described Ruby over the phone. Talk about an understatement.

Not that he could blame his sister for this situation. *He'd* been the one to hire the girl, sight unseen. He'd mistakenly assumed Ruby was a plain Jane, a homely thirty-year-old spinster who'd spent years looking after her dying mother and now wanted to become a social worker.

It wasn't Gloria's fault. Or Ruby's, for that matter. It was his own stupid fault for jumping to conclusions.

Thank goodness it was only a temporary situation. One day in the not too distant future, Georgia would be back and his life could get back to normal.

Meanwhile…

Sebastian heaved a deeply frustrated sigh before clenching his teeth hard in his jaw and heading downstairs.

CHAPTER FOUR

'RUBY, I PRESUME?'

Ruby's head shot up with a gasp, her eyes widening as she recognised the man standing on the back patio. It was Sebastian Marshall himself, whose images she'd looked up on the Internet just last night.

There was quite a difference, however, between them and the real thing.

First of all, she hadn't realised he was so tall. The photos had all been of him sitting down at a table on television awards night. She saw now that he was well over six feet. He was also even better-looking than she'd originally thought. Talk about tall, dark and handsome!

His photos hadn't done him justice, that was for sure. Then again, they'd all been taken at a distance and in profile. Up close and face on, he was gorgeous, with the kind of strong, manly features that aged well. No one would guess he was forty. His nose was straight and strong, his jawline very square and masculine with a small dimple in his chin. His dark brown hair was cut very short, showing ears that were set close to his head. There were a few lines around his mouth but they didn't detract from his well-shaped lips.

Ruby couldn't stop staring up into his very attractive face, and his even more attractive blue eyes.

So it was impossible for her to miss the narrowing of those eyes. Or the way he began frowning at her.

Automatically, Ruby clasped the towel she was holding to cover herself more modestly. Her bikini would not be considered risqué when worn on Gold Coast beaches, but it was possibly not the thing to be wearing on first meeting her new boss. She felt half naked, even more so since he was dressed in a business suit, complete with white shirt and tie.

'Goodness me, Mr Marshall!' she exclaimed as she stepped up onto the back patio. 'You frightened the life out of me. You said you wouldn't be home till tomorrow morning.'

'I caught an earlier flight,' he retorted in clipped tones. 'I sent you a text.'

'Really? I'm sorry but I'm sure I didn't get one. When did you send it?' she asked, determined to stay cool, and not become flustered.

'On my way home in the taxi. Clearly, you were in the pool at the time.'

For heaven's sake, she thought a little irritably. *That was a bit late to let me know you were coming home a day early.*

'Yes, I was,' she admitted. 'I've been in there for a while. It's been so hot. Look, I'll just dash inside, have a quick shower and get dressed. Then I'll make you some coffee, okay?'

She already knew from Georgia how much he liked

his coffee. And she knew how he liked it. Georgia had also told her that whilst their boss was long on looks he was short on charm.

Ruby could see what she meant.

'I won't be long,' she said as she hurried past him, shivering as her damp skin encountered the cool air inside the house.

Sebastian could not resist turning and watching her walk away from him, her peach-like derriere drawing his eyes, and holding them. Lord, but her body was delicious. Delicious and lush and so sexy it was criminal.

Sebastian suspected his sister had underplayed Ruby's looks because she didn't want to say anything to stop him hiring the girl. She was an incorrigible matchmaker, his sister, always plotting to find him a new wife. He recalled an argument they'd had not that long ago when he'd refused to come to any more of her infernal dinner parties where, naturally, there was always a single female seated next to him, just panting to give him whatever he wanted.

'I know you think I've been living the life of a monk since Jennifer died,' he'd thrown at his sister during that phone call. 'But you're wrong. Yes, I was celibate for a couple of years. Grief will do that to you. But I can assure you that when I want company, I get it.'

'But you never date anyone,' Gloria had argued back. 'You never *bring* a woman to my dinner parties. Or home to your place. Georgia told me. You're always alone.'

'It is possible to have sex without commitment these days, especially when you're travelling overseas and

interstate a lot and staying in five-star resorts and hotels. I don't have any trouble.'

'Well, bully for you. But is that all you want, Sebastian?'

'Yes, that's all I want,' he'd stated gruffly. 'I'm
not interested in falling in love again or having some
woman fall in love with me. I like my life the way it is.'

Which he did. He'd worked out a lifestyle that didn't
give him any grief, and he hated the thought of having
it messed with. He liked having a sensible middle-aged
plain woman as his housekeeper. He liked the feeling
of peace that greeted him when he came home each
evening. He liked living alone, free of potential pain
and emotional conflict.

He did *not* like the way he felt at this present moment. Not one little bit.

Sebastian swore, then stalked inside, feeling disgruntled, and, yes, very hot indeed. But he didn't go
upstairs and take his suit off. He just took his jacket
and tie off, undid the top buttons of his shirt and
headed for the kitchen, deciding not to wait for Ruby
to make his coffee. He would make his own. He was
in the process of doing so when she hurried into the
kitchen, dressed in black Bermuda shorts and a black
and white striped top, which had a boat neckline and
capped sleeves.

Admittedly, with her hair tied back and dressed in
ordinary clothes, she wasn't as distractingly desirable
as before. But nothing could stop the memory of how
she'd looked in that bikini, with her long dark hair
spilling over her shoulders. He was unlikely to ever
forget it, or what it did to him.

'You should have let me do that,' she said on seeing the coffee was well under way.

'It's all right, Ruby,' he replied, trying to make up in some small way for his earlier abruptness. 'I can make my own coffee.'

'But it's my job, Mr Marshall,' she protested. 'Here. You go and relax somewhere and I'll bring the coffee to you. I know how you like it,' she added with a smile that was as sweet and as perversely sexy as she still was. 'Georgia told me.'

When she came right up to where he was standing by the coffee machine, he caught a whiff of something tantalising. The scent wafting from her person was a mixture of coconut and vanilla. Not perfume as such. Possibly shampoo. Without thinking, he leant closer and inhaled, his nose not far from her hair.

Delicious, he thought once again. Everything about her was delicious. Delicious and dangerous and disturbingly tempting!

Gritting his teeth, he whirled around and strode away before he did or said anything seriously stupid. Ruby was, after all, his housekeeper. Which meant she was strictly off-limits.

So why was it that this thought didn't help dampen what was going on inside him? If anything, her being forbidden fruit made everything harder. Made *him* harder.

'I'll be in my study,' he called over his shoulder. Lord knew what he was going to do in there.

Get a grip! That's what you're going to do, Sebastian. Anyone would think you were a horny teen-

ager, not a forty-year-old man whose libido doesn't run his life.

Still, maybe I should have slept with that woman in London when I had the chance, he thought as he strode into his study and plonked himself down at his desk. Despite what he'd told Gloria, he didn't often indulge in casual sex, only when things got to a critical phase with his male hormones.

Clearly, things were getting to a critical phase, if he were to judge by his body's reactions to Ruby. Okay, she had a great figure and very sexy hair, but Sebastian was used to dealing with seriously beautiful women on a daily basis and, quite frankly, he never had a problem controlling himself around them. Yet the moment he'd laid eyes on Ruby in that bikini he'd got an erection the size of Centrepoint Tower.

Was it just a matter of intense frustration? Of going too long without sex?

He hoped so. Sebastian didn't like the thought that this attraction could be anything but a case of primal lust. To even contemplate anything else was emotionally disturbing, something which always brought with it a deep sense of alarm.

Emotional disturbances and Sebastian were serious enemies.

Thank goodness this was only a temporary annoyance, he reminded himself sternly for the umpteenth time.

CHAPTER FIVE

RUBY DIDN'T KNOW what to make of her new boss, despite Georgia having filled in a few of the pieces of the puzzle that was Sebastian Marshall.

'He's a workaholic,' she'd told Ruby over the phone. 'He lives and breathes Harvest Productions, with little time left over for socialising, unless it's to do with the business.'

When Ruby had asked about the lack of photographs in the house, Georgia had explained that Sebastian—Georgia called him Sebastian—had bought the house fully furnished five years ago and had not changed or introduced a single thing. She'd come with the house, the previous owners having moved overseas to work and sold off everything, including their housekeeper. Georgia said she hadn't minded as she liked working for Sebastian, who was often away and never brought women home.

'Never?' Ruby had asked, surprised.

'Never. His sister told me he never got over his wife's death. Apparently, she was the love of his life and died of cancer. About ten years ago, I think.'

'And there's been no woman since?'

Ruby found that hard to believe. A handsome man like that. And in the prime of his life.

'Not that I know of.'

Ruby wondered about that whilst she finished making the coffee. From what she knew about men—especially successful, good-looking ones—he wouldn't be doing without sex entirely. And if he'd been so devoted to his dead wife, why not put some photos of her around the house? It was as though he were trying to wipe out all memory of her.

The thought persisted that maybe her boss's marriage hadn't been as perfect as his sister imagined. People had believed her own parents' marriage had been great until the ugly truth came out. Her father had been cheating on her mother the whole time she'd been dying of cancer.

Ruby still found that reality hard to stomach.

Shaking her head, she picked up the coffee mug and headed for the study-cum-library, which was at the front of the house.

The door was shut. Ruby knocked.

'Come in,' came the snappy reply.

Ruby sighed, then entered. Sebastian Marshall was sitting behind his desk, a laptop open in front of him. He was staring at the screen, his upward glance both brief and almost dismissive. 'Thanks,' he said, his attention already back on the screen.

Ruby put the mug down by his right elbow then just stood there, waiting for his attention. His eyes eventually lifted to hers, and they were as cool as the air conditioning.

'Yes?' he bit out.

Ruby decided then and there to address his attitude, which she found unacceptable. Unacceptable and unnecessary. Georgia might put up with him being rude but she wasn't going to.

'Mr Marshall,' she began, then hesitated. When he looked at her like that—with hard narrowed eyes—her resolve weakened somewhat.

'Yes?' he persisted.

Ruby gathered herself and went on before she lost her nerve. 'I couldn't help but notice you were displeased to come home and find me in the pool. I was told I could use the pool when you weren't home and I had no idea you were coming home early. I'm sorry I didn't see your text but I never take my phone with me when I swim these days. Last time I did that I dropped it in the water and I had to buy a new phone.' Ruby knew her tongue was running away with her but, Lord, this man was seriously intimidating. Her heart was thudding in her chest and it was hard to hold his penetrating gaze. 'If you don't want me to use the pool at all,' she said, anxiety making her tone sharp, 'then please just say so.'

His sigh was heavy as he leant back in his chair and picked up his coffee, taking a sip before he answered.

'Of course you can use the pool, Ruby,' he said, then took another longer sip of coffee before putting the mug down. 'It wasn't you being in the pool that displeased me. Or you not reading my rather last-minute text.'

'Then what?' she asked, perplexed.

'May I be blunt?'

Was he ever anything else? 'Please.'

'You weren't what I expected…looks-wise.'

Ruby's heart sank. She'd come across a few employers in the past who'd not liked her looks, though they'd been mostly women. The men had never complained.

'I can't help my looks,' she bit out.

'Of course not,' he agreed. 'But you came as a surprise. Gloria said you were quite attractive but you're more than that, Ruby. Especially in a bikini.'

Ruby winced. She supposed that bikini was rather revealing. And whilst she didn't think her face was her fortune, she accepted that her figure was somewhat provocative when half naked.

'I promise I won't wear it again, Mr Marshall.'

'For pity's sake, Ruby, call me Sebastian. Georgia does. And of course you can wear your bikini. Just not when I'm home. And maybe not when I have visitors, which you'll find is reasonably often. Can I assume you know what I do for a living?'

'Yes. Barbara told me.'

He frowned. 'Barbara?'

'The woman who runs Housewives For Hire.'

'Oh, yes. Barbara. Then you know I'm in TV production.'

'Yes…'

'One of my shows is *Battle at the Bar*. I presume you've seen it?' he asked, and picked up his coffee again.

'Just the once,' she said.

'Really? Why just the once?' he demanded to know, banging the mug back down. Clearly, he was quite put out.

She shrugged, all the while trying to think up a reason why she hadn't watched one of the most successful shows on TV more often. 'I don't really like series,' she invented, 'especially crime ones with complicated storylines. If you miss an episode, you get a bit lost.'

'You can always catch up later online.'

'I suppose so,' she admitted, wishing she'd just told him the truth.

'*Battle at the Bar* has won a lot of awards,' he pointed out. 'You should watch it some more. Give it a chance to grow on you. Anyway, that's not why I brought it up. I just wanted to warn you that the star of the show—Zack Stone—often drops by. He's a good friend of mine but he's very fond of pretty girls. He'd probably try to make a pass at you given the chance. But you don't need to worry about him. I'll make sure he behaves himself.'

Ruby laughed. She couldn't help it.

His dark brows beetled into a frown. 'Why the laugh? I'm told he's irresistible to the female sex.'

'Not to me,' she said. 'I don't like men who think they're God's gift to women.' Or men at all much, if truth be told. She'd been through a wild phase when she'd first left home during which she'd gone to too many parties, drunk too much alcohol, and indulged in too much casual sex. She'd finally woken up to herself, however, and stopped before things got out of hand.

After that she'd sworn off men for ages.

But then she'd met Jason...

She'd been working as a receptionist in a hotel on the Gold Coast at the time, filling in for a girl who was away on maternity leave. He'd been a sales representative who stayed at this hotel very regularly. Jason had been movie-star good-looking with blond hair, blue bedroom eyes and buckets of charm to go with it. And he'd made a beeline straight for her.

Ruby had been flattered by his never-ending compliments, despite initially resisting his many requests to take her out. In the end she'd gone for coffee with him and then agreed to go to dinner with him when he was next in town. By then she was very attracted to him and possibly would have gone to bed with him. But thankfully, before he came back, she found out he was married.

To say she was crushed was an understatement, confirming what she already suspected about most men. They simply could not be trusted. But finding out the truth about Jason had the positive effect of turning off her libido entirely. She hadn't had sex for four years and didn't miss it one little bit.

'Just thought I'd warn you,' Sebastian said.

'Thank you, but you needn't worry. Zack Stone won't even get to first base with me.'

'Do you have a boyfriend already?'

'No. No boyfriend.'

'Girlfriend?'

She blinked her surprise at the question, one which no man had ever asked her before.

'No,' she replied.

'I probably shouldn't have asked,' he said, his smile wry.

When their eyes met and held for a long moment, suddenly, something like an electric current zapped across the space from his eyes to hers, revving up her dormant libido, tightening her stomach with the most amazing sexual awareness.

Dismay overwhelmed Ruby as she reached the stunning realisation that she just might want sex again after all. With this man. Her boss!

Ruby smothered a groan as she struggled to gather herself. But gather herself she did.

After all, wanting sex with Sebastian Marshall was only wanting, thank heavens. Ruby believed she could ignore it. Of course she could!

It was as well, though, that he didn't want her back. That much was quite obvious. His concern about her looks had not been personal. It had been professional. He'd been looking out for her, worried that his womanising star might make a pass at her.

'Is that all, Mr Marshall?' she asked, perversely irritated by his own lack of interest.

You should be grateful. Not annoyed.

'Sebastian, remember?'

'Right,' she said, and smiled a stiff smile. 'Is that all, Sebastian?' Lord, but he really was very handsome. And he had a very good body. Without his suit jacket on she could see the breadth of his shoulders. The top two buttons of his shirt were undone, giving her a glimpse of dark hair. She didn't mind a bit of hair on a man's chest. She actually found it sexy. Or she had, once upon a time.

Stop looking at him, she lectured herself. But where else could she look?

'Could you make dinner for eight tonight?' he said.

Ruby took a deep breath. She had to cook him dinner. Which was only logical. She was his housekeeper.

But she didn't want to cook him dinner tonight. She needed some time away from him, time to come to terms with the effect he was having on her.

'What would you like?' she asked, surprised at how cool she sounded. Yet she didn't feel cool inside. She felt all jumbled and jumpy.

'Surprise me,' he said and actually smiled up at her. Not a sexy smile. Just a polite one.

Ruby swallowed the huge lump in her throat, thinking that *she* was the one who was surprised. Though the word surprised didn't quite cut it. More like shocked. Stunned. *Shattered.*

Her dream job was turning into a nightmare.

Oh, dear…

CHAPTER SIX

'SOMETHING SMELLS NICE.'

Ruby spun round from the stove top, startled by her boss's sudden appearance in the kitchen. Startled, too, by his compliment. She tried not to stare, but he looked altogether different in casual clothes. Clearly, he'd showered and changed at some stage since she left him in the study a couple of hours ago. His dark hair was still damp, his tall, well-built body now housed in stone-washed jeans and a pale grey T-shirt.

Strangely, she preferred him in his business clothes, perhaps because it made him more out of her league. At the moment he looked like a guy she was allowed to fancy.

And fancy him she did. Big time.

'What are you cooking?' he asked before she could think of something to say.

'Beef stroganoff,' she told him matter-of-factly. 'Surely you've had beef stroganoff before?'

'Possibly. I'm not a foodie.'

'My version is hardly cordon bleu,' she said, wishing he would go back to his former rude self so she didn't have to secretly drool. 'I made it from a packet.'

'Well, it smells great.'

Ruby turned back to stirring, rattled by his unexpected pleasantness, not to mention her increasing awareness of him. Better she not look at the man any more than was strictly necessary. Talking was okay, as long as it wasn't accompanied by ogling.

'It was one of my brothers' favourite meals,' she threw over her shoulder. 'Along with spaghetti bolognese and a lamb roast.'

'I like the sound of all of those,' he said, that gorgeous voice of his making even the simplest compliment sound sexy. 'How many brothers do you have?' he asked, clearly intent on having a chat.

Oh, Lord, she thought, annoyed again by this totally unexpected attraction. Ruby wished he would just take his hunky body back to his study and wait there till she called him for dinner.

But no, that wasn't going to happen, was it? Out of the corner of her eye she saw him pull out one of the kitchen stools and slide onto it. If she was going to stay working for this man, she had no option but to turn round and answer him.

Clicking off the gas ring, she whirled around and dredged up a face that she hoped betrayed nothing but civility.

'Two,' she replied coolly. 'They're twins. Three years younger than me.'

The microwave pinged, letting her know the rice was ready. Good. Now she could serve him dinner and escape to her room.

'Identical?' he asked as she turned away to take the dish out of the microwave.

'No.' She placed the hot dish on a cutting board then looked up at him. 'But very similar. Do you want me to serve your dinner in the dining room or outside on the terrace?'

'I usually have dinner on a tray in my study when I'm alone here in the evenings. That way I can work or watch TV as I eat.'

Ruby should have guessed. Georgia had said he was a workaholic.

'That's fine. You're the boss. I'll just have to find a tray.' And she started rummaging around in the cupboards, banging a few doors as she did so.

Ruby hated the way she was acting. This wasn't like her. She was usually relaxed with people. But not with this man. He made her want to be stroppy. She hated that she fancied him. Hated that he made her heartbeat quicken by just being there.

She noticed him frowning, which in turn made her feel guilty.

'I think I need to apologise,' he said after she'd found a suitable tray.

'For what?' she replied, unsure what he was on about.

'For my attitude when I first came home. I had no right to imply that your looks could pose a problem. Or assume you couldn't handle yourself where Zack is concerned. I can see you're a very capable person who wouldn't accept unwanted attention from any man.'

Ruby was torn between being flattered and still annoyed. Not with him. With herself.

It was an effort to put aside her exasperation and find a small smile from somewhere. 'I have been known to put the odd man or two in his place,' she said, her voice still on the crisp side. 'You really don't have to worry, Sebastian. You're right. I can handle myself. But thank you for the apology. I admit I did feel upset that I hadn't made a good first impression on you.'

Sebastian did his best not to let his face reveal his re-action to her words. He'd come down to the kitchen to smooth things over, knowing full well that he'd been less than welcoming so far. Having a long, cold shower had helped with his frustrated male body, but there was no help for the memory of what had hap-pened when he'd first come home.

No, she *hadn't* made a good first impression. She'd made a very bad, very lasting impression, one that he suspected would torment him for the entire length of her time as his housekeeper. Not her fault, of course, but unfortunate just the same.

It had taken every ounce of his willpower to come in here and act the part of a boss for whom she might actually like to work, instead of the jerk she possibly thought he was. There was no doubt he hadn't made a good first impression on *her*, either. Sebastian was a reasonable judge of body language and he could see Ruby wasn't too happy with him. Which in one way was a good thing. But possibly awkward in the long run. If they were to coexist for the next few months, they had to establish a bearable working relationship. Sebastian had already decided to make himself scarce till Georgia came back but he couldn't be absent all the time. When he was home, however, he was determined to be polite, and pleasant.

'I'm sorry I made you feel that way,' he said. 'Let's start again, shall we?'

Her face showed that she was not going to be won over that easily. Her dark eyes flashed in a way that hinted at something close to annoyance, and her smile looked a little forced.

'But of course,' she agreed stiffly.

'Good. Now I'll just pop downstairs and get myself a bottle of red. I like wine with my meal at night.'

Sebastian was glad to escape down into his wine cellar where the air was almost as frosty as Ruby. His smile was wry as he pulled a bottle of his favourite Merlot from the shelves. If only she knew the R-rated thoughts that kept going through his head about her. No doubt she would quit on the spot.

Which might not be a bad idea. But he could hardly confess to the feelings that had rampaged through his body when he'd first sighted her in that damned bikini, and which he was only now getting under control. Because quitting would not be the only fallout to such a confession.

Sebastian had no intention of saying a single word on the matter, but the irony of the situation appealed to his sometimes dark sense of humour. He was still smiling when he reappeared in the kitchen.

Ruby, however, was not.

She had already set a tray with cutlery, a serviette and a wine glass. The correct wine glass for red, he noted. The only thing missing was the meal.

'Would you like a bread roll with your stroganoff?' she asked crisply.

'No. No dessert either.' Sebastian was suddenly tired of being accommodating. Or perhaps he was just tired. It had been a long and difficult day.

'How long will dinner be?' he asked.

'Not long at all.'

'See you soon, then.'

Swooping up the wine glass, he stalked off to his study. By the time Ruby arrived with the dinner tray he was already on his second glass. The alcohol hit his empty stomach hard, making him tetchy rather than mellow.

'Just put it down here on my desk,' he grumped.

'Right.' She put it down as ordered, her eyes speaking volumes. Clearly, he'd blotted his copybook again.

'What time would you like breakfast in the morning?' she asked in what could only be described as a cool voice. 'Georgia told me you like a cooked breakfast on Saturdays as opposed to weekdays when you just have coffee. She said you make the coffee yourself because you leave for work before most people are awake.'

'True,' he said, thinking Georgia made him sound like the worst kind of workaholic. 'I like to beat the traffic. But I actually won't need breakfast in the morning, Ruby. I intend to sleep in, then go out for brunch with some work colleagues. We have a lot of catching up to do after my trip. But I'll need dinner tomorrow night. At seven-thirty rather than eight. That spaghetti bolognese you mentioned will do fine.'

'Very well.'

'Did Georgia also mention you have Sundays off?' he asked, already looking forward to a day when she wouldn't be around.

'Yes.'

'Good. That's all for now.' As he dropped his eyes and picked up his fork, Sebastian was sure he heard her sigh. Not a big sigh. A small exasperated sigh. But he didn't look up. He just started eating, refusing to feel in any way guilty for his autocratic manner. He was, after all, not Ruby's friend. He was her boss. And Sebastian aimed to keep acting like a boss for the duration of her stay. That way, he might just stay sane.

CHAPTER SEVEN

RUBY BREATHED A sigh of relief when Monday morning came. Sebastian was up and gone with the dawn, leaving her with no one to please but herself for the day. Janice arrived at nine to clean, followed shortly after by the guy who picked up the laundry each Monday morning. Ruby had intended to help Janice upstairs after he left but was stuck downstairs answering phone call after phone call.

First there were her brothers, each making polite enquiries about the job, as well as asking her if she wanted to join them for Christmas lunch at the restaurant they went to every year and which required early booking. Ruby hadn't returned to Sydney for Christmas during the last five years and had been rather looking forward to a traditional Christmas at one of their places. She hated the thought of being the fifth wheel in their happy foursome and had declined their kind invitation, making some excuse about having to be on deck at the Marshall household.

Before she could surrender to guilt over this little white lie, Barbara rang from Housewives For Hire, wanting to know how she was getting along. No sooner had she finished with Barbara than Georgia rang with similar questions.

She told all of them the same thing: that she was fine, the job was fine, her boss was fine, and that she didn't foresee any problems. And brother, was that a *big* white lie!

Saturday had been sheer torture, especially after Sebastian came home around five and went swimming in the pool for over an hour. Which hadn't been too bad until he'd called out to her, asking her to bring him a towel, which he'd obviously forgotten. She had done as ordered, of course, which would have been okay if he'd stayed in the pool, but he'd chosen that moment to climb out.

Keeping her eyes off his hunky male body in those revealing trunks had been impossible. Lord, but he was one well-built man!

Hopefully, she'd hidden her feelings from him, feelings that she hadn't experienced in years. Not since Jason, who admittedly had stirred her female hormones somewhat. She'd been very attracted to Jason, but this thing with Sebastian was on another level entirely. This was nothing but sheer lust, as opposed to just attraction.

Ruby accepted ruefully that lust wasn't one of the seven deadly sins for nothing. Talk about tempting!

The only plus to the weekend was having Sunday off. She would have spent it visiting her brothers but they had both been having a weekend away at some hotel in the Blue Mountains, information she'd gleaned from Facebook, so she'd driven out to Parramatta where she'd spent the day in the mall, attempting to do some Christmas shopping. But not very successfully. She'd had trouble making up her mind so in the end had bought nothing. After that she'd gone to a movie, not arriving back at Mosman till late. Fortunately, Sebastian had been in bed by then.

Monday morning had come as a relief with Sebastian gone to work. Out of sight was out of mind! Though all that lying over the phone had put her boss firmly back into Ruby's thoughts again. After finishing with the phone calls, she had just put some coffee on when her phone rang again, her heart jumping when she saw it was Sebastian.

'Good morning, Sebastian,' she said, determined to act normal and not like the uptight creature she was in danger of becoming around him. After all, he couldn't hear her heart thumping away inside her chest, or see the X-rated images running around in her head, the ones that had plagued her after that incident by the pool.

'Hi,' he said. 'Everything okay with you?' he asked sharply, perhaps picking up some kind of vibe.

'Yes, of course. Everything's fine.' That word again. 'What's up?'

'Zack Stone will be coming over for a while this evening,' he announced. 'We'll need dinner.'

'Of course. What would you like?'

'Seafood. Half a dozen oysters each followed by barramundi and salad.'

Whilst Ruby admired a man who knew what he wanted, she was irritated by her boss's ongoing brusqueness. For a while there at the weekend he'd been nice and apologetic, but that hadn't lasted for long. 'What about dessert?' she asked.

'Something chilled. The weather's still damned hot and we'll be eating outside. Zack likes fresh air. Oh, and get a bottle of white wine from the cellar to complement. Actually, make that two bottles of white wine. I know I can trust you to pick well. I saw from your résumé that you've worked in plenty of restaurants and bars.'

'Indeed I have,' she said, thinking she'd met lots of men like him too. Talk about arrogant! But that was what came with men who were too rich, too good-looking and too successful. They simply couldn't help themselves. She supposed Zack Stone would be just as obnoxious.

'Anything else?' she asked archly.

'No. Oh, yes. I'm off to Surfers Paradise next weekend. I leave on Friday and won't be back till Monday so that leaves you free to do as you please over the weekend.'

Thank goodness, she thought. *Now I won't have to secretly ogle you all weekend. Or want to slap your face every five minutes.*

Unrequited lust, she'd come to accept, could make the sufferer extremely tetchy.

'Actually, that'll be great,' she said brightly. 'I have some studying to do. What are you doing in Surfers Paradise?' she couldn't resist asking. 'Business or pleasure?'

His hesitation to answer told her what she needed to know. People rarely went to Surfers Paradise for business.

'Just relaxing,' he said at last. 'Zack has an apartment up there which I use occasionally. It's not far from the casino. I enjoy playing Blackjack.'

Possibly he was telling the truth but Ruby doubted he'd be alone for long. Casinos were notorious pick-up places.

Ruby knew she had no right to be jealous, but she was all the same. She'd known instinctively that a man like Sebastian wouldn't do without sex. It wasn't natural.

A fantasy zoomed into her head in which he asked her to go with him…to spend the whole weekend with him. In bed, of course.

Just the thought excited her.

Not that he would ever ask her. Lord no! It was just a fantasy. Or possibly wishful thinking. It was obvious Sebastian was not the sort of man who did that kind of thing. Which was just as well. She'd come to Sydney to make an independent life for herself, not to fall into bed with her boss.

Get a grip, girl!

'Is Mr Stone going with you?' she asked, pleased to have herself under control again.

'That chick magnet?' he scoffed. 'Thankfully no. I'm just there for the gambling.'

'Of course,' she said, her comment having a decidedly dry edge to it.

He didn't say a word for several seconds. But when he spoke his voice sounded amused. 'I fear my new housekeeper is a cynic.'

'I fear you could be right,' Ruby retorted before she could think better of it.

'Good. Then you won't fall for Zack's charms.'

'Like I said before, Sebastian, I'm not a fan of that show, or its anti-hero.' Her voice was extra cool, a habit of Ruby's when a man assumed she was a pushover.

'Unfortunately, it's required viewing for all my staff,' he insisted. 'I get the best market research that way.'

'Really.' Thank goodness he didn't produce erotica, then, otherwise she might volunteer for more in-depth market research.

Ruby flushed at the way her mind kept going. Yet was it a flush of shame, or excitement? There was no doubt she was enjoying their repartee.

'What about your other shows?' she asked him.

'I'll give you a list tonight. They are *all* required viewing for employees of Harvest Productions.'

'That's a bit draconian, don't you think?'

'It's just for feedback,' he said.

'Oh, all right, then. Give me the list tonight and I'll look them up.'

'I'll do that. And I will appreciate your opinions, Ruby. You're obviously a very smart woman. Bye for now.'

Ruby hugged the compliment to herself as she hung up. Compliments about her intelligence had been in short supply in Ruby's life so far. Yet she *was* intelligent. She knew she was. Okay, so she hadn't covered herself with glory at school after her mother was diagnosed with cancer, and all her jobs so far had been on the menial side. But that didn't mean she didn't have a good brain.

It pleased her that Sebastian recognised she was

smart. And it pleased her, in a perverse way, that he wasn't bowled over by her so-called sexy looks. No woman wanted to be valued for her face or figure alone...though it wasn't a pleasant experience to be dead plain either, as she'd been as a teenager. Ruby hadn't blossomed until after her mother had died. She'd lost some weight and grown her hair, after which she'd finally snared her first boyfriend. Bailey, the rat.

She still wasn't conventionally pretty. But that didn't seem to matter. Men took one look at her and wanted her.

At least, a lot of men did. Clearly, Sebastian wasn't one of them. Which, she supposed, was good news. Yes, he recognised her attractions but obviously didn't feel compelled to act on them. Then again, there was clearly something wrong with him if Georgia had said he never brought a woman home. Never!

The man was a cold-blooded robot, Ruby decided. An emotionless machine. Either that or he was so damaged by grief over his wife's death, that he'd turned off his libido for good.

No, no, that wasn't right. If that was the case then he wouldn't be going away next weekend.

Ruby rolled her eyes, irritated with herself for thinking about the man so much. She had more important things to do. Like going shopping and buying fresh ingredients for tonight's dinner, along with something suitable to wear in front of a TV star.

CHAPTER EIGHT

'DO ME A FAVOUR, Zack,' Sebastian said as he approached his home. 'Try not to hit on my housekeeper tonight, okay?'

Zack threw him a puzzled look. 'And why would I do that? I never have before. Georgia is safe and sound.'

'I'm sure she is. But Georgia's in Melbourne, looking after her sister, who was in a car accident. I have a temporary housekeeper at the moment. Her name is Ruby. And she's a different kettle of fish from Georgia.'

'Really?'

'Yes, really. Younger. Attractive. And unfortunately single.'

'I see.'

'You don't actually,' Sebastian said ruefully. 'But you will.'

'So why am I getting warned off? You want her for yourself, is that it?'

Sebastian laughed. He couldn't help it.

'No,' he lied. 'You know very well I never get involved with my employees.'

'Or anyone else, for that matter,' Zack shot back.

'That's not true. I just like to keep my sex life away from home.'

'Far away from home, from what I've gathered. But we're getting off the point. Why aren't I allowed to chat this Ruby up? You said she was single.'

'She's also a *nice* girl.'

Now Zack laughed. 'Too nice for me, is that what you mean?'

'Yes,' Sebastian said, though he delivered the barb with a smile.

'Lovely,' Zack growled. 'My best friend thinks I'm a bastard.'

'I didn't say that,' Sebastian said, 'but you are a bit of a bad boy with women.'

Zack nodded. 'True,' he said. 'But it works for me, Seb. Bad boys often get the girl.'

'Yes, so I've noticed. Just not this time, please. Keep your bad-boy act buttoned up tonight and try to act like a good guy.'

'Fine. How boring.' His sigh was the melodramatic affectation of an actor. 'Very well. I guess I can channel my inner altar boy for one night.'

'Good,' Sebastian said as he angled into his driveway and headed down to the garages. Because he knew he couldn't stand it if Ruby fell for Zack's charm. And he could be charming. *Very* charming.

Sebastian's stomach tightened with tension as he made his way up the internal staircase, Zack hot on his heels.

'Is she a good cook?' Zack asked.

'Very,' Sebastian threw over his shoulder.

'That's good. I can at least enjoy the food, if not the company.'

Sebastian ground to a halt, then spun round to face his friend. 'What do you mean by that?' he demanded to know, his deep voice echoing in the cement-rendered staircase.

Zack's ruggedly handsome face creased into a wry smile. 'Can you hear yourself? You've been like a bear with a sore head all day.'

Sebastian sighed. 'Sorry. Business worries.'

'Like what? Your trip overseas went well. What have you got to worry about?'

'I guess I'm just a natural worrier.'

'That you are. You should be more like me. Nothing worries me.'

'So I've noticed. But we can't all be like you, Zack. Some of us actually have consciences.'

'Ah, so that's the problem. You do fancy this Ruby but you're her boss.'

Sebastian pursed his lips. To lie or not to lie? In truth he was sick of lying. And pretending. Last weekend had been hell. He shouldn't have come home early and even more stupidly gone swimming. Though it had seemed a good idea at the time. Then, to cap off his stupidity, he'd forgotten to take a towel with him. The way Ruby had looked at him when she'd brought him a towel—as if he was a complete idiot—was etched in his mind.

'Well, do you fancy her or not?' Zack prompted impatiently.

'I suppose I do,' he admitted at last.

'Then why didn't you just say so, for Pete's sake?'

'Because I don't *want* to fancy her,' Sebastian snapped. He didn't want to fancy *any* woman. That was the truth of the matter. After Jennifer's death he'd vowed never to become emotionally involved with another woman. Not as long as he lived.

Not that he was emotionally involved with Ruby. Lord, no. He felt sure he knew exactly what was eating away at him. It was nothing more than lust. Though given she was living in his house, that could develop into a dangerous situation as the weeks went on.

'Thankfully, she's only my temporary housekeeper,' he ground out. 'In a few months, she'll be gone. In the meantime…'

'In the meantime?' Zack asked with raised eyebrows.

'I would prefer not to think of her in your bed.'

Zack smiled. 'I can appreciate that. Nothing worse than the object of your affections being seduced by another man.'

'She is *not* the object of my affections. Just my hormones.'

'Then perhaps you should do something about those hormones. Oh, yes, you already are, aren't you? That's why you're off to Surfers next weekend. Plenty of hot babes up there.'

'You'd know,' Sebastian said.

Actually, getting laid wasn't his chief reason for going away. He just wanted to put some distance between himself and Ruby. He certainly didn't want a repeat of last weekend. Of course, if some hot babe made a line for him, it might be wise to succumb.

Though, damn it all, sleeping with anyone other than Ruby did not appeal.

He was damned if he did and damned if he didn't.

Sebastian's sigh held frustration. 'I suggest we get ourselves inside before Ruby wonders where we are.'

CHAPTER NINE

RUBY HAD BEEN wondering where they were for some time. She'd heard Sebastian's car go down the drive, followed by the whirr of the garage doors, and she'd expected them to make an appearance shortly afterwards. But a few minutes had gone by and still no show. The door from the stairwell remained steadfastly closed.

The delay did nothing for her sudden attack of nerves.

Racing down to her bedroom, she checked her appearance, one glance in the wall mirror bringing a satisfied sigh to her lips. She wasn't wearing any make-up tonight but her olive skin and her dark, heavily lashed eyes did not suffer from a lack of enhancement. And the black shirtdress she'd bought, thinking it was perfect housekeeper fare, somehow didn't look as dowdy and plain as she'd hoped. It did, in fact, look very smart.

She sprayed her hair, which was trying to escape the tight bun she'd imprisoned it in. Feeling more confident, she thought, *If that actor bloke tries to chat me up, I'll put him in his place, quick-smart. I'm good at that!*

No sooner had she finished with her hair than she heard Sebastian calling out to her from the kitchen.

'Ruby, where are you?'

'Right here,' she said as she hurried from her room, smoothing down her skirt with clammy hands on the way.

Sebastian's guest looked her up and down, his icy blue eyes showing curiosity rather than lechery. He really was an attractive man, but not a patch on Sebastian, who was seriously handsome. In her eyes, anyway. She adored the way her boss looked tonight in his grey business suit, especially with that white shirt and red tie. Zack, on the other hand, was wearing jeans and a black singlet top, which showed off his heavily tattooed arms. His dark brown hair was too long, in Ruby's opinion, and rather messy, whereas Sebastian's dark brown hair was always superbly groomed in that short-back-and-sides cut, which she liked. Sebastian looked like a gentleman whereas Zack looked every inch a bad boy.

'Nice to meet you, Ruby,' Zack said when Sebastian introduced her, 'Sebastian has been speaking highly of you. Says you're a great cook.'

Goodness, she thought. No smarmy comments, or long meaningful gazes. Just normal eye contact and polite compliments.

'That's nice of him,' she said, relieved. 'I'm okay but no cordon bleu chef. I hope you like seafood.'

'Of course he does,' Sebastian said, not looking at her at all as he removed his jacket and tie. 'I wouldn't have asked for it, otherwise. Come on, Zack, we'll have a pre-dinner drink in my study. Ruby,' he added with a quick look her way, 'let us know when you're ready to serve.'

And just like that they were gone, leaving Ruby wanting to strangle Sebastian for she knew not what. For not fancying her, she supposed. Still, she figured she should be grateful that Zack Stone wasn't going to be a pest this evening.

But she didn't feel grateful for anything at that moment. She just felt peeved, even more peeved when she called the men to dinner half an hour later and neither of them said anything about the table, which she'd gone to great pains to set beautifully.

By the time Sebastian complimented her on her choice of wine she was in no mood to be gracious. Her smile felt forced, her movements as she set the oysters down in front of them decidedly brisk.

'Glad you like it,' she said, then retreated to the kitchen before she showed her displeasure.

They disposed of the oysters quite quickly but seemed happy to sit and drink the wine till the main course was ready. The evening had turned balmy after the suffocating heat of the day. The sky was clear above and the stars had come out. Not that Ruby took much time to look at them. She was too busy cooking the barramundi, which was not an easy fish to get just right. Nothing worse than overcooked fish.

Luckily, it all turned out well. Sebastian's guest was especially complimentary. The walnut salad and fresh bread rolls she served with the barramundi were also a hit, even with Sebastian, which went some way to improving Ruby's mood. A more genuine smile lit her face as she removed their empty plates.

'How long before you want dessert?' she asked when she saw Sebastian open the second bottle of wine, which had been chilling in the ice bucket next to the table.

'Leave it for half an hour,' he told her, and was in the process of pouring them both a glass of wine when his phone rang.

'Damn it,' he growled. 'Should have turned it off.'

'You can always let it go to voicemail,' Zack said.

'Better not. It's my sister. She wouldn't actually ring me unless it was important.'

Ruby had a sudden premonition that somehow this phone call would affect her, and not in a good way. She wasn't sure how till Sebastian rose to his feet.

'I'll take it inside,' he said, and left her alone with Zack.

Uh-oh, Ruby thought as she cast their visitor a wary glance.

'Sit down, Ruby,' the man himself said and gestured to the chair adjacent to him. 'Would you like a glass of wine? You've done nothing but work all night. And possibly all day, by the look of this table.'

'No, I don't want any wine,' she told him, and made no move to sit down.

Zack smiled. 'No need to stress,' he said. 'Your boss has already given me strict orders not to try anything. He thinks you're far too nice for a bastard like me.'

'Oh!' she exclaimed. 'How rude of him to say such a thing!'

'Maybe, but he's quite right. You *are* far too nice for a bastard like me. Now, go and get yourself a glass.'

Ruby decided then and there that she liked Zack Stone. She didn't lust after him, however, which was just as well since he had a charm that she could see would be dangerous to the wrong woman.

When she returned with a glass and sat down, Zack didn't fill the glass straight away. Instead he reached out and took hold of her wrist—not in a lecherous way—and turned it over.

'Who's Ava?' he asked as he stared at the small heart-shaped tattoo.

'My mother,' she replied thickly.

He frowned at the dates before letting her wrist go and looking up at her.

'You must have been young when she died.'

'Nineteen,' she admitted, then waited for him to ask more questions.

But he didn't.

'My mother died when I was young too,' he said at last. 'But not as young as you.'

'Please don't tell Sebastian,' she said quickly, glancing over her shoulder lest her boss suddenly reappear.

'Why not?'

Ruby sighed. 'It's complicated.'

'Fair enough. We all have our secrets. And yours is harmless enough. Let's have some wine.'

Ruby was glad for the conversation to move on. Glad too of the soothing effect of the alcohol. It still amazed her how upset she could get when she thought of her mother's death. Though maybe it was her father's behaviour at the time and afterwards that kept her distress alive. Men could be such bastards.

She stared at Zack over the rim of her wine glass and wondered what his secrets were. Something deep and dark, she suspected. But any musings about her guest were cut dead by Sebastian stomping back to the table, his face grim.

'Well, my weekend at Surfers is off,' he growled as he slumped into his seat and swept up his wine glass.

'Why?' Zack asked before Ruby could. 'What's happened?'

'My mother's birthday is what happened. It's next Saturday. Gloria was going to take Mum out for the day but her doctor husband has to go to some medical conference in Adelaide and he wants her to go with him. Which means yours truly has to do the honours.'

Ruby rolled her eyes at him. 'Is that all?' she said as she rose to her feet. 'You should be thankful you have a mother.'

He did look a little shamefaced at this comment. 'Yes, yes, I know that. But she's just so difficult to please. Never likes anything on restaurant menus. She used to drive my father mad when he was alive. He liked interesting food. But not Mum. She prefers the plainest fair.'

'Then why not bring her here and I'll cook her something she likes?' Ruby suggested before it sank in that it would be better if he took his mother out for the day. The whole day!

'What a good idea,' Zack said. 'This is a great girl you have here, Sebastian.'

Ruby could have sworn that Sebastian threw his

friend a decidedly caustic glance. Ruby realised he was probably thinking Zack was trying to butter her up.

Sebastian sighed. 'Thank you for the offer, Ruby. That's very kind of you.'

His warm compliment brought a sudden flush of heat to her whole body.

'Time for dessert?' she asked, her voice going a little high, as it did when she was agitated.

'Absolutely,' Sebastian said. 'What is it?'

'New York-style cheesecake. What do you want with it, ice cream or cream?'

'I'll have ice cream,' Zack said before Sebastian answered. 'And plenty of it. This damned heat is getting to me.'

'It's supposed to storm tomorrow,' Ruby told him.

'Good.'

'Not good,' Sebastian snapped. 'We're shooting outdoors tomorrow.'

'I'm sure we'll cope. It might add some atmosphere to the episode if it rains. The way it is, that scene is a bit bland.'

Sebastian frowned. 'You think so? I thought it was intense.'

'It didn't read that way to me.'

'Why didn't you say so earlier?'

'I would have, but we were discussing other things, remember?'

Ruby decided it was time to go. 'Sorry to interrupt, but what do you want with *your* cheesecake, Sebastian?'

He stared at her for a long moment before a wryly amused smile quirked the corner of his mouth. 'I'll have what Zack's having,' he said, bringing a laugh from Zack.

'Very funny, Seb.'

Ruby didn't think it was funny, the quote from the well-known romantic movie causing her mind—and her body—to zing with the type of sexual tension that was difficult to ignore.

Ruby knew there would be nothing fake about her orgasms if she ever went to bed with her boss. Not that she ever would. But it was still a struggle to focus on the present moment and not some ridiculous fantasy.

'That reminds me,' she said, looking straight at Sebastian with a cool, businesslike expression. 'You didn't give me the list of your shows like you said you would.'

'Sorry. I forgot. I'll get my PA to email you the list and the screening times tomorrow.'

'Right,' she said, and went to get the desserts, feeling ridiculously hurt that he'd forgotten. It was silly really. Very silly. But then this whole business of being attracted to Sebastian was silly. He wasn't interested back. Yet, in that perverse way of human nature, this only seemed to make him even more attractive to her.

Ruby had spent the last few years fending off the attentions of the male sex. It was ironic that the one man she wanted to want her, *didn't* want her.

She supposed she should be grateful for that. Sebastian wanting her would have caused trouble in the end because she would have been faced with the dilemma of working women everywhere. Should she or shouldn't she?

Sleeping with the boss was never a good idea. *Never!*

Nevertheless, it was a wickedly exciting idea when Sebastian was the boss in question. Ruby should have been shocked at herself for even thinking about it. But she did think about it. Endlessly. And she wasn't shocked. She was aroused.

Oh, dear, she thought as she spooned the ice cream onto the plates of cheesecake, stuffing a big spoonful into her overheated mouth at the same time.

Do try to cool it, Ruby. You're on a good wicket here. Don't do anything to spoil it!

'This looks delicious,' Zack said when she put his dessert in front of him. 'Did you cook it yourself?'

'No. I bought it from this wonderful bakery not far from here. It's where I got the bread rolls from too.'

'A good bakery is worth its weight in gold,' Zack said. 'So is a good housekeeper,' he added. 'You're a lucky man, Sebastian.'

Sebastian's lips pressed grimly together as he cast his friend an exasperated glance.

'I do know that, Zack,' he bit out. 'Ruby is a find, that's for sure. That's all for now, thank you, Ruby. We won't have coffee. We'll just finish off this wine.'

'Okay,' she said, and traipsed back to the kitchen, not sure whether or not she was pleased with all those compliments. There was something…odd…about them, as though Zack and Sebastian had some secret agenda going on involving her. She couldn't think what. Maybe it was all in her imagination. There was a lot going on in her imagination, all of it about Sebastian.

Ruby stacked the dishwasher slowly, her head going round and round with frustrating thoughts. When she heard the men come in from outside and walk towards the front of the house, she returned to clean off the rest of the table. She heard the front door bang shortly afterwards and was in the process of making herself some coffee—which didn't keep her awake like most people—when Sebastian made an appearance. Alone. Clearly, Zack had taken a taxi home.

'Did Zack make a nuisance of himself when I was taking that call?' were his first words.

Ruby turned from the coffee machine to eye her grim-looking boss. Lord, but those blue eyes of his could go quite dark when he was angry.

'Not at all,' she replied. 'He was very nice. Quite the gentleman, really.'

Those eyes narrowed further, his high forehead bunching into a frown. 'You *like* him,' he said, almost accusingly.

'Yes, I do.'

'I did warn you about him.'

'Sebastian, stop,' she said firmly. 'I like Zack, but not in that way.'

'I find that hard to believe. Most women drool over him.'

'Then I'm not most women. I assure you, he's not my type. On top of that, I'm just not interested in men at the moment.' Just one man in particular. 'I've come back to Sydney to study for a degree. I want a career, not a boyfriend. Men cause complications.'

'You don't want to get married?'

'No. Marriage is not for me.'

His head tipped to one side as he studied her. 'Why is that, Ruby?'

'That's a very personal question,' she told him with more than a touch of anger.

It brought him up short. 'You're right. It's none of my business. I apologise.'

'Accepted. Do you want coffee?'

'God, no. I've already got enough to keep me awake tonight. By the way, thanks for offering to cook dinner for my mother next Saturday night. That was very kind of you.'

Their eyes met and Ruby's heart melted with that squishy feeling she always got when anyone talked about kindness, and mothers.

'My pleasure,' she said thickly. 'Do you know what foods your mum likes most?'

'Not really. Give Gloria a ring tomorrow and ask her.'

'I'll do that.'

A rather long look passed between them, a look that had Ruby's heart pounding behind her ribs.

'Is there anything else?' she asked at last, just to break the awkward silence.

'No,' he said brusquely. 'I'm off to bed to try to get some sleep. I have an extra early call tomorrow. Goodnight.'

And he was gone, leaving Ruby to stare after him with a mixture of longing and curiosity. What a strange man he was. One minute caring about her welfare, the next dismissing her abruptly. She decided then and there that when she spoke to his sister tomorrow, she would try to find out a little bit more about him, and about his late wife.

CHAPTER TEN

'RUBY!' GLORIA EXCLAIMED. 'How nice to hear from you. I hope there's nothing wrong.'

'No, no,' Ruby replied. 'Unless you count the rain. Isn't it strange? We were all dying of the heat and praying for rain, then when it comes, it's annoying.'

'I know exactly what you mean. Janice was complaining about it this morning. Said she hates having to use the dryer all the time instead of hanging the washing out on the line.'

For a split second, Ruby wondered why Gloria was talking about Janice's washing, till she remembered Janice was Gloria's cleaner as well as Sebastian's.

'I don't have a clothes line here,' Ruby said. 'I send all the washing out, as per Georgia's instructions.'

'Lucky you.'

'They do a brilliant job, I have to admit. And it saves me a lot of ironing. Anyway, Gloria, the reason I'm calling is because I've offered to cook your mother a special birthday dinner here on Saturday night and I wanted to find out what sort of food she liked.'

'Goodness! That's brave of you. Mum's hard to please where food is concerned. I usually take her to a buffet where she can pick what she likes. She's very fussy.'

'Perhaps I should give her a call and ask her personally what her favourite meal is.'

'Actually, I think that's an excellent idea. Her number's in your house phone, under Frieda Marshall.'

'Right. So is there anything else I should know about her?'

Gloria chuckled. 'So much I don't know where to start. Just make sure the table setting is pretty and use the dining table inside. She hates insects almost as much as she hates the heat.'

Ruby frowned. 'You make her sound like a grumpy old woman.'

'She's not. Not really. Just hasn't got enough to think about. But she'll love this personal attention. Trust me on that. Thank you so much, Ruby. You're very thoughtful.'

'Just trying to help my boss out really. He seemed in a bit of a panic about it all.'

'Really? That doesn't sound like Sebastian.'

'Perhaps panicky is an exaggeration. More like put out that he couldn't go to the Gold Coast for the weekend.'

'He was going up to the Gold Coast for the weekend?'

'He *was*.'

'He never said. What was he going there for?'

Ruby realised this was the opening to find out some more information about Sebastian but the words got stuck in her throat. Which was just as well, for it would sound as if she was prying, and Gloria was no fool.

She would put two and two together and conclude that Ruby fancied Sebastian. Which, unfortunately, she still did.

'I have no idea,' Ruby said with feigned indifference. 'I'd better go and ring your mum. I'm off to the supermarket later and I'll want to know what to get.'

After they said their goodbyes, Ruby rang the number for Frieda Marshall straight away.

'Hello?' came the slightly quavering answer.

Gosh. She sounded as if she was ancient. Yet she couldn't be all that old. Seventy perhaps?

'Is that Mrs Marshall? Mrs Frieda Marshall?'

'Yes,' she replied in the same wobbly voice. 'Who's this? You're not Georgia.'

Ruby realised that Georgia's name must have come up on the caller ID. She was, after all, using the house phone.

'No. I'm Ruby. Sebastian's new housekeeper. Georgia was called away to a family emergency and I'm standing in until she gets back.'

Frieda gasped. 'A family emergency? What kind of family emergency?'

Ruby explained the situation, all the while amazed that Sebastian hadn't thought to tell his mother what had happened.

'Poor Georgia,' the woman murmured. 'And poor Sebastian. He'll be lost without her. Who's going to organise his firm's Christmas party? It's not long till Christmas.'

'That's all under control,' Ruby informed her, thankful that it was. 'Georgia booked the caterers in advance and all I have to do is make sure the house is clean.'

It took Ruby a good five minutes to worm out of Frieda what she would like for her birthday dinner. What she wanted—she said rather sheepishly—was rissoles.

'Rissoles?' Ruby echoed, thoroughly taken aback.

'Yes. Beef rissoles,' Frieda said eagerly. 'And mashed potatoes. Lovely creamy mashed potatoes. The cook here is all right but her mashed potatoes are always lumpy.'

'I make good creamy mashed potatoes,' Ruby told her with a catch in her throat. It had been one of the foods her mother had been able to manage when she was on chemo. Ruby closed her eyes for a long moment before blinking them open again.

'And what about dessert?' she went on. 'Any favourites there?'

'I really shouldn't eat dessert. I've put on a few pounds lately.'

'But you must have dessert. It's your birthday. Come on, Mrs Marshall, it's your special day. You deserve a treat.'

'Oh,' the old lady said with a happy sigh. 'What a lovely thing to say. All right, then,' she went on, sounding less trembly now. 'I adore lemon meringue pie and I haven't had one in years. Do you think you could buy one somewhere?'

'Buy one? I suppose I could try, but I'd prefer to make one fresh.' Ruby was confident she could find a recipe on the Internet.

'Are you sure? I know they're a bit fiddly to make.

My mother used to make them when I was a girl and she always complained.'

'I'm a good cook, Mrs Marshall. I'll cope.'

'You are kind. And do call me Frieda.'

'Thank you. Much better than Mrs Marshall. Now, what time do you like to eat, Frieda?'

'Not too late. I get tired.'

'Would you rather have lunch?'

'No. I like the idea of dinner.'

'Okay. What say I get Sebastian to pick you up at five-thirty? You can have a pre-dinner drink with your son, then dinner will be ready at six-thirty. How's that?'

'Sounds perfect. But you might have to buy some sherry for my pre-dinner drink. Sebastian won't have any. He never has any.'

'I'll get some in. What kind of sherry? Dry, sweet or cream?'

'Cream.'

'And what would you like to drink with your dinner?'

Frieda hesitated before answering. 'Er...could you buy a bottle of spumante? Sebastian won't have any of that in the house, either.'

No, he wouldn't. Ruby could see by his cellar that he was a bit of a wine snob, like most wealthy men. They looked down their noses at drinks like spumante.

'Any particular brand?' she asked.

'No. Any bottle will do. They all taste the same, don't they?'

Ruby knew this wasn't true and decided to buy the most expensive.

'Can you think of anything else you might like, Frieda?'

'No, not really. I've already given you a lot of work. But thank you so much.'

'My pleasure. I'll see you Saturday, then.'

'Saturday. Yes. Oh, how exiting. I'll have to go and tell the girls. Bye, love. And thank you again.'

Ruby stood still for a long moment after she clicked off. Love. She'd called her *love*, which had been her mother's favourite endearment.

Oh, dear…

Ruby forcibly straightened her shoulders then went to pick up her tablet to look up recipes for lemon meringue pie. The rissoles she could manage with her eyes closed—her brothers adored rissoles—but the pie might have to have a dry run on Friday because she wanted everything to be perfect for Frieda, and not just because she was Sebastian's mother, but because it was her birthday. And everyone deserved to be spoiled on their birthday.

CHAPTER ELEVEN

RUBY WAS IN the fresh vegetable aisle of the supermarket when her phone rang. Her heart jumped when she saw the caller identity. Jumped, then raced.

'Sebastian,' she answered with creditable cool. 'Hi.'

'Hi to you too. I've just had a call from my mother. She said you rang and asked her what she'd like to eat on Saturday night.'

'Yes, I did. Is there a problem with that?'

'No, of course not. She was very complimentary about you. Said she prefers you to Georgia.'

'Really?'

'Yes. Really.'

'What about you?' Ruby asked cheekily before she could think better of it. 'Do you prefer me to Georgia?'

His hesitation gave her the answer to her stupid question. Or it did until he sighed.

'You both have different qualities, Ruby. Georgia certainly never cooked my mother a birthday dinner. As I said last night, you're a very kind person.'

Ruby was glad he couldn't see her blush this time. Or the way his compliment affected her.

'She's sweet, your mum. By the way, how old is she?'

'Seventy-three. Why do you ask?'

'She sounded fragile,' she said. Or she had, at first.

'That's a bit of an act,' Sebastian said. 'She's as healthy as a horse.'

'I see. Still, I did wonder why she wasn't living with you. It's not as though you don't have the room.'

Sebastian's laugh was dry. 'My mother would never live with me. She says I'm a misery guts. Not to mention a workaholic. She told me she'd be talking to the walls after a while, since I'm never at home.'

'Oh. What about Gloria?'

'God, no. Gloria has two teenage boys. Mum couldn't stand the noise.'

'Have either of you actually offered?'

'We both did and she refused. Look, she likes living in the retirement village. She has lots of friends there. Now stop playing the social worker, would you?'

'But I wasn't!'

'Yes, you were, Ruby. I suspect you're an incorrigible fixer. Trust me when I say my mother is happy where she is.'

Ruby pulled a face at this, knowing full well that his mother wasn't *that* happy. If she was she wouldn't have been so grateful for Ruby offering to cook her a special birthday dinner.

'Now on to my real reason for this call,' Sebastian swept on before Ruby could think of a suitable comeback. 'I realised this morning that I'd forgotten to talk to you about the Christmas party I throw for my staff every year. It's booked for Friday next week. I'm worried it might be too late to hire the party people we usually use.'

'You don't have to worry,' Ruby said. 'Georgia already had that organised. She booked the caterers well in advance. She told me they bring everything, do everything, and even clean up afterwards.'

'Good old Georgia.'

'She's certainly very organised. So how many people are coming to this party?'

'A lot.'

'Twenty? Thirty? More?'

'At least fifty.'

'Wow. That is a lot. So who will be there?'

'Are you fishing to find out if Zack is coming?' he asked sharply.

Ruby suppressed a sigh. 'Not at all. Is he coming?'

'I would imagine so. Speaking of work matters, I also just remembered that I forgot to get that email sent to you about the times of my shows. Sorry. I'll get my PA to do it, asap.'

'Please don't. I really don't have time to watch much television at the moment, Sebastian. I have a lot of studying to do.'

'Already? I wouldn't have thought any course would start until well after Christmas.'

'That's not the case with online courses. They start when you want them to start. I will find time to watch *Battle at the Bar*, but not the others.'

'Okay. The latest episode airs this Friday. You can tell me what you think on Saturday at breakfast.'

'I'll be glad to. So, what do you want for dinner tonight?'

'Didn't I tell you? I won't be home for dinner any night this week.'

'No, you didn't tell me,' she said, feeling quite put out. Yet she should have been grateful. Out of sight was out of mind, right?

On the other hand, absence also made the heart grow fonder...

Don't be silly, Ruby, she lectured herself. It's not your heart involved here. It's something much more basic.

'More time for me to study, then,' she quipped. 'Anything else you've forgotten to tell me?'

The sudden silence down the line unnerved her until she heard him clearing his throat.

'You sound like you're catching a cold,' she said.

'Could be. I hate the rain. Have to go now, Ruby. If I don't see you before I'll see you on Saturday morning at breakfast. I'm looking forward to hearing what you thought of Zack's show.'

'I'll take notes,' she said brightly. No point in giving away the fact that she would miss his company, even if his presence frustrated her like mad.

His sigh sounded weary.

'Are you all right, Sebastian?' she asked.

'Yes. Like I said, we're having a few problems with this last episode. But nothing that can't be fixed, I hope. Bye.'

'Bye,' she returned, but he was already gone, leaving Ruby with a strangely heavy feeling in her chest.

CHAPTER TWELVE

By Friday, the rain that had dogged Sydney all week had finally begun to clear. Sebastian's sexual frustration had begun to clear as well, intense work and several days away from Ruby's provocative presence doing the trick. But that hiatus was now over and he had to face the weekend ahead, with all its accompanying difficulties.

The thought of bringing his mother over for a home-cooked dinner tomorrow was not something Sebastian was looking forward to. His mother would take one look at Ruby and think what Gloria had probably thought when she first met her. That she was wife material.

He wished his mother and sister would abandon the hope that he would marry again one day. Because he wouldn't. They simply didn't understand his resolve after Jennifer's death never to risk a serious relationship with a woman again. The truth was he simply could not bear to go through what he'd gone through ten years ago. It had scarred him for life, time not having dimmed the feelings that welled up within him every time he thought of Jennifer dying like that.

He shuddered whenever he thought of falling in love again, of leaving himself vulnerable to such pain. Lust he could cope with, but not love. It bothered him how much he already liked Ruby. He would have to be careful around her. Very careful.

Sebastian took some time to fall asleep that Friday night, despite the late hour he'd come home, late enough for Ruby to be safely in bed. He woke on Saturday morning with a start, his head turning to stare at the pillow next to him, a tortured groan punching from his throat.

Ruby wasn't there, of course. It had all been a dream, a wildly erotic dream where Ruby had been lying naked in his bed with her gorgeous hair spread out across the pillow, her eyes glazed from hours of lovemaking.

The trouble was he could remember the lovemaking so very well—though one could hardly call it lovemaking. It had been nothing but sex of the raunchiest kind. Primal even. He'd been a beast. A crazed beast. Not like him at all. But it had thrilled him to the core, and left him to wake up still cruelly aroused.

Groaning, he opened his eyes and swung his legs over the side of the bed.

Such acute physical frustration bothered him enormously. He wasn't used to it. After Jennifer died he hadn't wanted sex for a couple of years. Then, when his male hormones had finally demanded he listen to them, it hadn't been with this kind of intensity. He'd been able to satisfy his sexual needs by having the occasional fling when he was away from home.

He could have been away from home now, he thought irritably, having his sexual needs met.

But he wasn't. He was here. And his needs were staring him in the face. No doubt his arousal was mainly because of that damned dream, but also partly because he'd be seeing the object of his desires this morning. There was no avoiding Ruby. No escape. Today was going to be hell, starting with breakfast.

Oh, well. No use putting off the inevitable. He had to face his nemesis sooner or later. But first he determined to do something about the dreadful state he was in.

Gritting his teeth, Sebastian hauled himself onto his feet and headed for the bathroom.

It was five past nine before Sebastian made an appearance in the kitchen, Ruby's spirits lifting at the sight of him.

'There you are,' she said. 'I was beginning to think you weren't ever going to come home.'

He said nothing to this, instead picking up the newspaper, which was delivered every Saturday and which she'd placed on the breakfast bar.

A silence descended as he attempted to remove the plastic cover, giving Ruby the opportunity to observe him stealthily. He looked tired but still handsome, casually dressed in fawn chinos and a white T-shirt. His dark hair was still wet from the shower and his face unshaven, which was unusual for Sebastian. His grooming was usually perfect. Yet the stubble suited his masculine face. And added to his sex appeal.

Unfortunately.

'What do you want for breakfast?' she asked after he succeeded in freeing the paper of its stubborn confines.

'A tall glass of orange juice to begin with,' he answered, finally looking up at her. 'Then a couple of poached eggs on toast followed by lots of coffee. I'll eat outside,' he finished up.

'Right,' she said through gritted teeth. For whilst Ruby was getting used to his on-off brusqueness, it still offended her. Why couldn't he just be nice?

Lord knew why he put her libido in such a twist. She didn't really *like* him all that much, but it seemed lust was not necessarily connected with liking.

He didn't go outside straight away. Instead, he just stood there on the other side of the breakfast bar, frowning at her old jeans and the very large apron that covered her from neck to knee.

'Yes, I know,' she said with a defensive shrug of her shoulders. 'I look a fright in this apron. But I've been cooking pastry, which can be messy. Don't worry, I'll look decent by the time your mother comes.'

'I'm sure you'll be perfect,' he bit out, spinning on his heel and stomping outside.

It was at moments like this that Ruby didn't just dislike him. She *hated* him. But then he spoiled everything by smiling at her when she brought the juice outside.

'Sorry for being grumpy,' he said. 'It's been a tough week.'

'That's all right,' she said, and smiled back at him before she could stop herself.

Their eyes met over the rim of the glass and her

heart turned over. Dear God. As much as she wanted to keep hating him, she just couldn't. He wasn't a hateful man. Not even remotely.

'So did you watch *Battle at the Bar* last night?' he asked after he took a huge swallow of juice.

'I did.'

'What did you think of it?'

'It's an exceptional show,' she said truthfully, glad to have something to distract her from her escalating feelings for this man. 'I doubt there's anything else like it on TV at the moment. It hooks you in within five minutes and keeps you on the edge of your seat for the whole hour and a half. The story last night was riveting and Zack was just brilliant. If ever I get into trouble with the law, I'd want someone like him in my corner.'

'He is good, isn't he?'

'Better than good.'

'Why do you think that is? I sometimes try to work out what appeals to people about him so much. Is it just his looks, or his acting? Or both?'

Ruby considered her answer for a few moments, aware that Sebastian was watching her. Watching and waiting. 'I think it's the passion of the character he plays,' she said at last. 'Caesar *cares* about his clients and he shows it. Of course,' Ruby added, 'it does help to have a strong plot, not to mention all that sex.'

'True. Sex sells,' Sebastian said, then drained the rest of his juice. 'Thank you for that very intelligent critique, Ruby. Could I have the eggs now?' he asked as he picked up the newspaper and started reading.

She had been dismissed.

Ruby wanted to scream. Or hit him. Or both.

Instead, she turned and started to walk back inside, holding her temper with great difficulty.

'What about the coffee?' he called after her.

Ruby stopped, then turned back round to find him folding the paper up and putting it down. 'You said you wanted it *after* your eggs,' she pointed out tartly.

'Did I? Well, I've changed my mind. I'd like it now.'

'Coming right up,' she said through gritted teeth.

It was a good ten minutes after that she brought him the coffee before she returned with his eggs, her mood still dark.

'Ah,' he said, looking down at the eggs. 'This looks so good. Thank you, Ruby.'

Ruby stifled a sigh. He'd done it again. How did he disarm her when she was mad at him?

'So, did Gloria drop by yesterday with the presents for Mum?' he asked before he started eating.

'Yes. I put them on the dining table, ready for her.'

'Good. I have to go out after breakfast so I won't need any lunch. I have a meeting with the writers of Zack's show, then I'm taking them out to lunch as a thank you for all the extra hours they put in this week.'

'They fixed the problems, then?'

'Yes. They got it right in the end, which is just as well. Nothing worse than a season ending on a bad note. You have to end on a high.'

'I would imagine so,' she said thoughtfully. 'You… er…you won't be late home, Sebastian, will you? Your mother will be upset if you're late picking her up.' She didn't add that *she'd* be upset if tonight didn't go well, after all the work she'd done.

'No, Miss Worrywart,' he said as he picked up his

knife and fork. 'I'll be back in plenty of time to get ready for tonight's ordeal.'

'It doesn't have to be an ordeal,' she chided him.

The corner of his mouth lifted in a wry smile. 'That's a matter of opinion.'

When he dropped his gaze and began to tuck into his eggs, Ruby realised she'd been dismissed again.

One day, she thought frustratedly as she made her way back to the kitchen, *I'll tear strips off that man.*

What Ruby didn't realise was that that day had already arrived.

CHAPTER THIRTEEN

Sᴇʙᴀsᴛɪᴀɴ ʀᴇᴛᴜʀɴᴇᴅ ᴛᴏ the house shortly after four-thirty, disappearing straight upstairs without even bothering to say hi. Ruby faintly heard the sound of his shower running. And running. And running.

Truly, she thought as she shook her head from side to side. Just as well he was rich. His water and electricity bill must be enormous!

She herself had already showered and dressed some time ago, choosing to wear her black shirtdress. *Again*. Still, it did look good on her. Her make-up was subtle and her hair imprisoned in a knot at the nape of her neck. The house was spotless, the dining-room table set with pretty new place mats, and all the food prepared, including that infernal lemon meringue pie, which had turned out to be a real pain in the neck. She'd tried three recipes during the week, only the third one meeting with her approval. Even then, she'd had Tom and Janice do a taste test yesterday on a trial pie. Thankfully, it had met with their approval, so she'd given the rest of that pie to them to take home and made a fresh one this morning; Ruby had read that meringue was better consumed on the day it was made.

She was a little nervous about the evening ahead, but excited as well, glad that she could make the day memorable for Sebastian's mother.

He hurried downstairs shortly after five, cleanly shaven and dressed in stylish navy-blue trousers, teamed with a blue striped shirt, open at the neck. He looked refreshed and utterly gorgeous, but with a grim set to his mouth, which suggested he wasn't looking forward to the evening ahead.

'I hope your mother doesn't live too far away,' she said, glancing at the clock on the wall.

'Don't fret. She's less than ten minutes away at Clifton Gardens. In a very *exclusive* retirement village, I might add. It costs me heaps. I should be back by five-thirty, as long as she's ready and doesn't keep me waiting. See you.'

And he was gone again, leaving behind the faint whiff of a very expensive cologne. Or possibly it was aftershave. Either way, it smelled wonderful.

Ruby took another deep breath through her nose, wallowing in the fragrance. There was nothing she liked better than a man who smelled good.

Some extra butterflies started gathering in her stomach when five-thirty came and went, with no sign of Sebastian. She hoped nothing had gone wrong. Ruby was just beginning to panic when she heard his car enter the driveway. She was busying herself with plates in the kitchen when the door from the stairwell opened and Sebastian ushered his mother inside.

Frieda looked nothing like her son. She was short and plump with a kind face, topped by a cap of wavy silver-grey hair. Her dress was very flowery and didn't flatter her plump figure, but her white shoes and handbag looked expensive, especially her handbag. Ruby had a thing for handbags and could always recognise quality.

'Happy birthday,' Ruby said by way of a greeting, coming forward to give the woman a hug, then a kiss on her cheek.

Frieda flushed with pleasure before throwing her son an exasperated glance. 'You didn't tell me Ruby was so pretty. And so *young*!'

Sebastian rolled his eyes. 'She's not as young as she looks,' he said.

'Well, she's a darned sight younger than Georgia.'

'True. Come on, Mum, come and open your presents.'

The dining room was just off the kitchen, a large conservatory-style room with a lovely view of the pool, the backyard and the skyline beyond. The table wasn't overly huge though it did extend, if needed. Ruby had set only one end of the table with two place settings, the presents piled up on the other end and a vase of fresh flowers in the middle.

'Goodness!' Frieda exclaimed. 'That's a lot of gifts.'

'They're from Gloria as well,' Sebastian told her. 'And your grandsons.'

Frieda opened the cards first, then the presents. She was quite overcome at one stage.

The range of gifts was extensive, including an expensive tablet, jewellery, a lovely scarf, books and chocolates. The tablet was from Sebastian, though Ruby suspected he hadn't done the buying. Clearly, he'd delegated that job to his sister.

Still, his mother didn't know that. Or maybe she did, because she said she would have to ring Gloria straight away and thank her.

Whilst she was on the phone, Ruby asked Sebastian what he would like to drink before dinner.

'I think I'll have a whisky. But don't you worry. I'll get it myself.' And he took off down the hall towards his study where Ruby knew he kept a wide range of spirits on top of a walnut sideboard.

'Ready for a sherry now?' she asked a teary-eyed Frieda once she got off the phone.

'Oh, yes, I could do with one. Where's Sebastian?'

'Getting himself a whisky.'

'Let's hope it improves his mood,' Frieda said with a sigh.

'Yes, let's,' Ruby returned, and both women exchanged a small smile.

'I shouldn't criticise him,' his mother said, taking her glass of sherry. 'He's really a good son. Do you know about his wife dying of cancer?' she whispered, all the while watching for Sebastian's return.

'I do,' Ruby said, nodding.

'It broke his heart.'

'Yes, I can see that.' And she could.

'I hoped he would meet someone else and get married again. But he doesn't want to.'

Ruby could see that too. It shouldn't have bothered her, but it did. Which was crazy. It wasn't as though *she* wanted to marry him. Heavens no. She just wanted to…

Her X-rated thoughts weren't entirely banished when Sebastian strode back into the room, a glass of whisky in his hand. When he lifted it to his lips, her eyes followed, her heart quickening. What she wouldn't give to be that glass of whisky…

'Excuse me, I need to go and cook now,' she said quickly. 'Why don't you two go outside with your drinks? It's lovely out there at the moment. The rain has chased away the heat and the insects. I put some nibbles on the table earlier. I'll call you when dinner's ready.'

They did as instructed but when Ruby finally called them inside, Frieda took one look at the two place settings and insisted Ruby eat with them.

'Maybe she doesn't want to, Mum,' Sebastian said when Ruby hesitated.

'Don't you have enough food for three, dear?'

'Yes, I do. But I… I'm not family.'

'Nonsense. You *feel* like family already, doesn't she, Sebastian?'

Ruby experienced some sympathy for her boss at that moment. His mother had really backed him into a corner. He looked totally frustrated with her, his eyes carrying exasperation before he finally surrendered, a small rueful smile playing on his lips.

'Yes,' he said. 'She does. Please, do join us, Ruby.'

Surprisingly, the evening went quite well, especially after she brought out the bottle of spumante, which Frieda consumed with gusto. The rissoles and mashed potato went down a treat but the *coup de grâce* was the lemon meringue pie, served with whipped cream. The gushing compliments from Frieda made all the trouble she'd taken worthwhile. Ruby hummed as she made the coffee, warmed by the feelings she always got when she made people happy, confirming her decision to become a social worker.

Frieda lingered longer than Ruby expected. She wanted to chat with Ruby a lot, asking about her life and her travels. Not that Ruby told her the whole story—more an edited version of it. After all, Sebastian was listening. Listening intently, she noted, and watching her with the sort of narrowed eyes that might have indicated interest on another man. But not Sebastian. He was just curious about her, she decided. Not attracted.

It was just after ten when his mother announced it was time she went home, with Sebastian obviously eager to take her. Ruby sensed he'd had enough.

'This is the best birthday I've ever had,' Frieda praised as they gathered up all her gifts and carried them down to the car. 'What a shame Ruby won't be here next year,' she added. 'Are you sure you can't fire Georgia and keep her, Sebastian?'

A look of horror flickered across his face before he could hide it. 'Afraid not, Mum,' he replied. 'But she'll be with us a while yet.'

'Yes. Yes, I suppose so.' Frieda looked disgruntled for a moment, then her face brightened. 'You'll have to bring Ruby to Gloria's for Christmas Day. Gloria always does a turkey with all the trimmings.'

Now *that* was the sort of Christmas celebration she liked.

'Ruby might have other plans, Mum,' Sebastian said before she could jump at the invitation. 'She has family here in Sydney.'

'Actually, I don't have other plans,' Ruby said truthfully. 'I'd love to come. If that's all right with you, Sebastian. And Gloria, of course.'

Their eyes met, his betraying nothing. Nothing at all. It annoyed the hell out of her that he didn't find her even a little bit attractive. But then, perhaps he didn't find any woman attractive these days. Maybe that was why he never brought a woman home. Because his libido was dead and buried, alongside his wife. Clearly, she'd been the love of his life and he had no room in his heart for anyone else. Maybe he *had* only been going to the Gold Coast to relax.

But even as Ruby worked through these thoughts, she wasn't entirely convinced. For she had been aware of *something* simmering between them tonight. Women did have good antennas about these things. And hers had been twanging all night.

But maybe she was wrong. Maybe it was her own stirred hormones twanging away. In truth, she hadn't been able to stop looking at him surreptitiously as she'd chatted away with Frieda. Looking at him, and wanting him. This lust business—especially when it was one-sided—was a right pain in the—

'I'm sure Gloria would love to have you,' Sebastian said briskly, putting an end to her musings. 'Now, come along, Mum. You said you were tired.'

'Thank you again, dear,' Frieda said, coming forward to give Ruby a goodbye hug.

Ruby was glad when they left. She, too, was quite tired. It didn't take her long to finish clearing away the table and put on the dishwasher. Ruby decided not to wait for Sebastian to come home before having her shower and going to bed. He wouldn't expect her to.

She was just about to dive in between the sheets when there was a knock on her bedroom door. Her stomach tightened with instant alarm.

'Yes?' she called out warily.

'Are you decent?'

Ruby glanced down at the elongated T-shirt that she wore to bed. It was white with a colourful beach-side logo on the front, which hid her underlying nakedness to a degree. But not entirely. Nipples like bullets were hard to hide. She reached for her blue cotton house-coat, pulling it on and wrapping it around herself as she walked to the door.

'Yes?' she repeated once the door was open.

To give him credit, he did look at her for once like a normal man, his eyes going from her released hair down to her bare feet. But once his eyes returned to hers, there was nothing there but cool politeness. 'I just wanted to thank you personally for all the trouble you went to today. You went above and beyond the call of duty.'

'My pleasure,' she said, dismayed and, yes, disappointed. Which was silly. What had she been imagining? That he'd come to her bedroom to seduce her at long last?

She wished.

'Mum thinks you're lovely,' he said.

Ruby's smile was stiff. 'That's nice.'

'I think you're lovely too...'

It was all so unexpected. Ruby was shocked, both by the sudden thickness in his voice and the unmistakable hunger that zoomed into his eyes. When his desire-filled gaze dropped to her mouth, she sucked a breath in sharply. For surely he was going to kiss her. Any second now, he was going to step forward, pull her into his arms and crush his lips down on hers.

A wave of longing—no, *craving*—swept through her. For it was what she wanted more than anything else in the world. Ruby knew it wouldn't stop at kissing. She couldn't *bear* it to stop at just kissing. She wouldn't *let* it stop at just kissing.

'Sebastian,' she said, the uttering of his name filled with her own hunger. She had never in her life felt anything as intense as the desire gripping her body right now, not to mention her mind. There was no room in her head for any other consideration. No thought of common sense, or consequence. No care for the future, just the here and now, and this utterly overwhelming need.

He stared at her hard for several seconds, his eyes glittering with the same need. Then, suddenly, he shuddered and turned his back on her.

'Goodnight, Ruby,' he threw over his shoulder, and started to walk away.

CHAPTER FOURTEEN

Ruby was stunned. For a split second she just stood there, staring after him, until a fury rose within her. It wasn't the fury of a woman scorned. It was the fury of a woman crushed by the disappointment of him rejecting what was clearly a mutual desire. There she'd been all this time, thinking he didn't want her. But he had. He *had*!

Yet despite this, he was walking away…

It was too much.

'Don't you dare walk away from me!' she exploded.

He stopped and turned back to face her, his expression disbelieving.

'I beg your pardon?' he bit out.

'You heard me,' she retorted.

'I thought I must have been mistaken,' he said coldly. 'So what's your problem?'

'*My* problem,' she threw at him. 'I don't have the problem here. *You're* the one with the problem. I can't work out if you're some kind of masochist, a sadist, or a coward.'

His nostrils drew together as he sucked in sharply. 'I would think carefully before you say any more, Ruby.'

She tried to rein in her temper but she simply couldn't.

'Good grief, what's wrong with you? Are you going to deny the way you looked at me a minute ago? Trust me when I say I know that look. You wanted to make love to me. And I wanted you to, more fool me. I was ready to jump into bed with you just like that,' she said, clicking her fingers at him. 'I was yours for the taking. But what did you do? You bolted.'

His eyes darkened to a stormy blue, his hands curling into fists by his sides. 'I was trying to be a gentleman,' he ground out. 'More fool *me*. But you're wrong about me wanting to make love to you,' he went on grimly. 'I didn't want to do *anything* to you that smacked of love. I wanted to have sex with you, Ruby. I wanted to ravish you senseless. That's why I walked away. Because I knew a nice girl like you wouldn't want that.'

Now it was her turn to suck in sharply.

His admission was not only surprising, it brought with it a measure of guilt, plus a huge wave of temptation. Ruby knew she should step back and think about the consequences of what she was about to say, but she was beyond that. She wanted Sebastian on any terms.

'You're wrong about me,' she said, desperate with desire for him. 'I'm not as nice as you think. I've had sex without love in the past. Please don't walk away, Sebastian. Not tonight. I need you, just as much as I think you need me.'

'I doubt that,' he muttered. But he didn't walk away. Instead, he covered the distance between them with a few swift strides, sweeping her up into his arms just as she'd imagined earlier, his mouth swooping down to crush hers.

His kiss was savage, his lips demanding. But, oh, how she loved it, opening her mouth to the thrust of his tongue, her body already aching to feel the thrust of hard maleness pressing up against her stomach.

The kissing continued as he wrenched the housecoat off her shoulders, his hands dropping to her thighs, taking the hem of her T-shirt with them as they travelled up to her bare buttocks. There he cupped her bottom, kneading the soft flesh till she was moaning into his mouth. He didn't stop kissing her, even when he lifted her up; didn't stop as he carried her upstairs to his bedroom. Once there, he tipped her back onto the bed, spreading her legs and leaving her exposed to his gaze as he stripped off his clothes.

Ruby just lay there like that, stunned by her level of arousal. She wasn't used to this kind of need. This degree of wanting. This kind of sex.

She could hardly wait.

And neither could he, by the look of him. Once he was naked, her arms reached out to him and he fell into them, groaning as he did so. He entered her swiftly, his thrusting urgent but, oh, so satisfying. Ruby came with a rush, stunned by the intensity of her orgasm, calling out his name as the first spasm struck. He stopped for only a second to stare down at her before returning to his frantic rhythm. His climax was just as strong, his body shuddering at length. Finally, he collapsed upon her, his head buried in her hair.

His ragged breathing took ages to calm, by which time Ruby's whole body had surrendered to a deeply drugging peace. The craving was gone, at least for the moment. Before she could think, or experience any regret, she fell fast sleep, oblivious to the not so nice feelings that would face her when she awoke.

CHAPTER FIFTEEN

SEBASTIAN WOKE FIRST, shocked to find himself still on top of a sleeping Ruby.

Oh, dear God, he agonised. *What have I done?*

He groaned as he carefully withdrew, then, without looking back, he headed for the shower. There he stood under the jets of hot water for ages, his head pressed against the tiles, his thoughts whirling.

He should never have gone to her door last night, should never had said those stupid words.

I think you're lovely too...

Of course, he hadn't expected her to react the way she had when he'd walked away. My goodness, she'd been furious with him. And the things she'd said, the things she'd accused him of being...

What were they? A sadist, a masochist and a coward.

Sebastian knew he wasn't a sadist. But he had to admit that he'd suffered from a degree of masochism ever since Ruby had come to live with him. He'd been permanently aroused whenever he was around her. Last night, the dinner with his mother had been sheer torture, having to sit there and watch Ruby all evening, watch her and want her.

He hadn't imagined for a moment that she was as attracted to him as he was to her. She'd certainly hidden it well. But the moment she'd revealed her own hunger for him he'd been lost. Totally lost. He could still feel her lips, her tongue, her hot, wet body.

Sebastian hadn't experienced that kind of passion since…since *never*, he suddenly realised. Sex with Jennifer had never been wildly spontaneous like that. It had been good. Of course it had. But there had always been an element of control. On her part. Not his. She'd liked to put aside special times for lovemaking. She'd never indulged in a quickie. Never been so overcome with desire that she couldn't wait.

Thinking back, Sebastian accepted that whilst Jennifer had loved him, she'd never really *needed* him. Not in life, or in death. But that hadn't made losing her any easier.

That brought him to Ruby's last accusation. That he was a coward.

Sebastian sighed. Maybe there was an element of truth in that accusation. After his experience of losing Jennifer, Sebastian had withdrawn into a shell from which he hadn't emerged for a long time. Even then he hadn't been able to consider a relationship with another woman, settling for one-night stands and the occasional holiday fling. He'd always kept these encounters well away from home, so that nothing could come back to haunt him.

Sleeping with Ruby broke all the rules he'd been living by.

Common sense demanded that he ask her to leave. But how could he possibly do that? Maybe, just maybe, he wouldn't have to. He suspected Ruby might do the deed for him and just quit.

And maybe she wouldn't. Sebastian obviously found it hard to read her because she'd shocked the life out of him last night. Thinking about her explosive passion still amazed him.

Sebastian snapped the taps off and reached for a towel, dismayed when he noticed he was already aroused again.

'Hell on earth,' he muttered under his breath as he wrapped the towel firmly around his waist then reached for the bathroom door.

He found Ruby sitting on the edge of the bed, her shoulders slumped, her head bowed. Her head jerked up when she heard the door open, distress in her eyes.

'I suppose I'll have to quit now,' she said.

Such a prospect did not sit well with Sebastian, which was perverse, given he'd already decided it would be easier if she quit.

'I'm so sorry,' she blurted out before he could say a word. 'It's all my fault. I know it is. You tried to walk away but I wouldn't let you. I provoked you. I don't know why. No, that's a lie. I do know why. I wanted you to make love to me. No, that's a lie as well. I didn't want you to *make love* to me. I wanted you to have sex with me the way you said. You know? Nothing to do with love at all. And you did. And I loved it. I really did,' she choked out, then burst into tears, her head dropping into her hands.

Sebastian couldn't bear it, seeing her cry like that,

and accepting all the blame. He rushed over and sat down next to her, wrapping an arm around her shaking shoulders and drawing her close to him.

'You just needed sex the same way I did. I dare say you haven't had any for a while, have you?'

She shook her head from side to side. Was that a yes, or a no? Did he care either way? Probably not.

'Same here,' he said. 'Now stop crying and let's talk about this situation like sensible adults.'

Hopefully, he could manage that, though he suspected that what was under his towel might influence what he had to say. Thank goodness she was still wearing that T-shirt. If she'd been sitting there naked, he wouldn't have stood a chance of a rational conversation.

Ruby looked up at him with wet eyes. 'I need to go to the bathroom first and freshen up.'

'Freshen up,' he repeated before the penny dropped. He hadn't used a condom—another one of his rules broken. Oh, God…

'Now I'm the one saying sorry,' he said, sighing. 'I should have used a condom. Let me assure you that's a first for me so you don't have to worry about STDs. What about birth control? Are you on the pill?'

'Yes,' she said. 'Though I'm not sure why. It's been years since I had sex. Now I really *have* to go to the bathroom.'

He stared after her, stunned by her announcement that it had been years since she'd had sex. No wonder she'd liked it so much. Still, he couldn't help wondering what had happened in her past to make her choose a celibate lifestyle. Especially looking the way she did. She certainly wouldn't be short of admirers.

But he had no intention of asking her. Sebastian didn't want to know all about Ruby's life story. The intimacy he craved was of the strictly sexual kind. Lord, but he had to have her again. And soon.

An idea leapt into his head that seemed feasible, though very un-Sebastian-like. He was, at heart, a conventional man. And a careful one. Not that you would think so by the way he'd just acted. The idea was outrageous, he knew, but once it infiltrated his thoughts, he could not put it aside.

Would she go for it? He sure as hell hoped so.

Sebastian climbed into bed whilst she was gone, his body urging him on, despite some lingering misgivings over what he was going to propose. He would have to make it clear to her up front that his proposition was to be a strictly sexual arrangement. No emotional involvement. Just sex. And it would all end when Georgia came back.

Ruby emerged after a few minutes, looking worried. And hesitant. When she saw his towel on the floor beside the bed, her eyes widened.

'Are you expecting me to join you in there?' she asked him.

'Only if you want to.'

She pulled a face. 'That's not fair, Sebastian. You know I want to.'

'Then what are you waiting for?'

She walked round and climbed into the bed on the other side but kept a bit of distance between them.

'Okay. I'm here. You said you wanted to talk about

the situation like sensible adults, though I can only assume by your invitation to join you in bed that you don't want me to quit.'

Sebastian had to smile. No flies on Ruby. 'You're absolutely right. I want you to stay on as my house-keeper. But we crossed a line tonight, Ruby, and I'm afraid it's impossible for me to step back over that line. Do you know what I'm saying?'

'Yes. You want to have more sex with me.'

'Yes. I do. And I promise I'll use protection from now on. What do you say?'

Her smile was small and wry. 'I think I could suf-fer it.'

'Good,' Sebastian said, trying to keep a straight face. She really could be a saucy minx. This was some comfort, as was her admission to having had sex be-fore without love. 'There will, however, be conditions to this affair.'

'*Conditions?*' she asked, her frown indicating she wasn't all that happy with that word.

'Maybe conditions is the wrong word.'

'You could be right there,' she said sharply.

'I shouldn't have called it an affair, either, because it won't be that. It will be an arrangement.'

'An arrangement,' she repeated, as though mulling that word over as well. Sebastian began to feel as if he was tackling this all wrong.

'Look, I'm sorry,' he said. 'I'm expressing myself badly. But the truth is I don't want a girlfriend, Ruby, just you as my lover. I also don't want anyone else to know, or guess, that we're sleeping together.' When his conscience pricked at him, Sebastian steadfastly ignored it. 'What do you think of that idea?'

'Wow,' she said, though she was still half frowning. 'So you want me to be your secret lover?'

'I couldn't have put it better myself,' he said with a relieved sigh.

'Wow again. That's a very daring proposition for a gentleman like you, Sebastian. I mean, you're not a bad boy like Zack. What's got into you?'

'I don't think you have to look far to know the answer to that,' he said, and closed the distance between them. 'You've totally undermined my common sense, along with my conscience,' he added, lifting the T-shirt up over her head and tossing it away. 'So is it a yes, Ruby?'

CHAPTER SIXTEEN

HE KISSED HER before she could answer, one hand covering her left breast at the same time. When she finally came up for air, her head was whirling.

'Er...could you give me some time to think about it?' she asked, wondering all of a sudden whether she was capable of conducting a strictly sexual affair without that soft heart of hers finally getting involved. She didn't want to fall in love with Sebastian. She really didn't. To do so would be futile. And ultimately bring her a lot of grief. Common sense demanded she leave things at a one-night stand and just walk away.

But common sense was no match for the exquisite feelings pulsating through her body at that moment. Already his hand had moved from her breast down between her legs to that area that was pulsating and throbbing.

'How much time do you think you'll need?' he asked, and stopped what he was doing.

'I'm not sure,' she squeaked, desperate by now.

'I need an answer, Ruby.'

'Yes. All right. Yes.'

'Do you want me to continue?' he murmured knowingly.

'Please,' she moaned.

Her orgasm shattered any lingering qualms Ruby had about saying yes. For how could she give up such pleasure? And if it worried her that she would get emotionally involved with Sebastian, or that he would say goodbye to her without a backward glance when Georgia returned, she pushed such thoughts aside. Because already he was inside her, taking her with him to a level of satisfaction she'd never experienced before. She came and she came, her body shattering into a million pieces of pure pleasure. By the time she fell asleep with his arms tightly around her, Ruby's mind had moved beyond something as mundane as worry. She was totally obsessed. With this man, with his body, and the way he could make her feel. She would do anything he asked of her if it meant she could be with him.

The sun was well and truly up when Ruby woke the next morning. Sebastian was still out like a light, which didn't surprise her. He'd outdone himself last night, leaving her feeling exquisitely sated.

What did surprise Ruby, however, was that she was having second thoughts about this…arrangement she'd agreed to. Really, what had possessed her to say yes just like that?

Of course, she *knew* why she had at the time. But that didn't make it acceptable in the cold light of day. Pride demanded she talk to Sebastian about it again, make some *rules* of her own. She wasn't about to be at his sexual beck and call whenever he felt like it, even if being at his sexual beck and call did hold a decidedly wicked appeal.

Ruby cast a glance over at his sleeping form, images popping into her head of the various activities they'd indulged in during the night. She had to admit he was very good at oral sex. She also hadn't shrunk from going down on him, either, even though it had never been one of her favourite forms of foreplay. With Sebastian, however, it seemed she was up for anything.

And she meant *anything*!

Her stomach twisted with renewed desire, bringing with it the temptation to just stay here in this bed till Sebastian woke up.

But if she did that, Ruby feared she would be lost. She had to have some self-respect. She had to make a stand.

You've never been the meek and mild type, she lectured herself, *and you're not about to start now. Now get out of this bed and put some distance between yourself and this infernal man.*

Ruby crawled out very quietly lest she wake Sebastian. Because if he touched her she just knew her resolve would crumble. Once out of the room, she hurried downstairs, collected some fresh clothes and bolted for the nearby bathroom.

She lingered in the shower, shampooing her hair whilst letting the hot water soothe her body, though there was not much soothing for her mind. It was once again a total shambles.

Some loud knocking on the bathroom door brought an end to her tortured thoughts.

'Ruby, how long are you going to stay in there?' Sebastian demanded to know. 'You've been in that shower for ages.'

Now, there was nothing more guaranteed to make Ruby defiant than a demanding man. Who in hell did he think he was?

Ruby snapped off the taps so he could hear her answer, loud and clear.

'Might I remind you, Sebastian, that it's Sunday, which is my day off. I have plans. So if you want coffee, then I suggest you get it yourself. Now, if you don't mind, I'd like to be left in peace to finish my ablutions.' And she turned the taps back on again.

Ruby thought she heard a four-letter word through the hiss of the water. It brought a wry smile to her lips. Yes, this was the way to play it. She couldn't be at his command all the time. A girl had to have some pride.

It was fifteen minutes later before she emerged, dressed in her favourite black Bermuda shorts and a simple red T-shirt. Her still-wet hair was bundled up on top of her head in a rough knot. She had no make-up on and no shoes on her feet. This she swiftly remedied, slipping on black thongs before padding her way down to the kitchen where Sebastian was sitting on one of the breakfast stools, a mug of steaming coffee in front of him.

'I see you did as I suggested,' she said, trying not to stare at him. It was obvious he was naked underneath the short black silk robe he was wearing.

'I've never minded making my own coffee,' he returned, his eyes glittering with a desire that she found both perturbing and tempting.

'How generous of you,' she said.

He looked at her long and hard. 'You don't like men much, do you?'

'Depends on the man,' came her truthful reply.

'What about me? Do you like me?'

A small smile tugged at her mouth before she could stop it. 'You're growing on me.'

'You're an enigma, do you know that?'

'What do you mean?'

'I can't work you out.'

'Do you have to? I'm your temporary housekeeper. And your secret lover whilst I'm here. End of story.'

'Is that what you expect? That once your time here is over, then we're over?'

Her smile turned wry. 'Of course.'

'And you're okay with that?'

She shrugged, doing her best to ignore the sharp tug at her heartstrings. 'Yes. Of course.'

His face showed a perverse mixture of relief and exasperation.

'When I woke this morning and found you gone, I thought you might have changed your mind.'

This was her chance to say, *Yes, I've changed my mind. I quit and I'm out of here before I do something stupid like fall in love with you. Because there is no future in that. Even if you are actually a nice man. But you don't want love and marriage. You don't want anything from me but sex. Which I thought was all I wanted from you but now I'm not so sure...*

'I couldn't bear it if you changed your mind,' he said, half to himself.

Ruby's heart turned over as she accepted that it was

already happening to her. The caring. The emotional involvement. She'd always been a sucker for being needed. And Sebastian needed her. At least for a while.

The time for walking away was gone, Ruby accepted bravely. She'd made her bed, so to speak. Now she would have to lie in it.

She laughed at the irony of that thought.

'What's so funny?' he asked, frowning.

'Nothing important. One thing, though, don't think I'm going to jump into bed with you every time you get the urge. I don't belong to you.'

Obvious relief smoothed the frown lines from his forehead. 'Well, of course you don't, Ruby. I don't always act like a beast, like I did last night.'

Ruby thought she'd better not tell him she'd rather liked that beast.

'Do you mind if I ask you a couple of questions?' she said.

An immediate wariness zoomed into his face. 'That depends on the questions.'

'Were you happy in your marriage?'

'Very. Why?'

'You don't have any photographs of your wife around the house.'

'No,' he said grimly. 'I don't like to remember.'

'Your happiness together, or her dying of cancer?'

'I would imagine you already know the answer. You've been there, Ruby. You know what it's like.'

'Yes. It's very difficult,' she said, her heart going out to the bleakness in his eyes. 'But I don't think it's wise to try to blank it all out. See this?' she said, and showed him the tattoo on her wrist. 'Ava was my mother. I had this done so I would never forget her, or the love I felt for her.'

Sebastian studied the tattoo, then looked up at her, frowning. 'But the date of her death... You said she died five years ago.'

'No. I said I left home five years ago. You just assumed that was when she died.'

'Why did you let me think that, then?'

'It's a long story. Are you sure you want to hear it?'

CHAPTER SEVENTEEN

SEBASTIAN SUSPECTED HE SHOULDN'T, but he couldn't resist. His curiosity was well and truly awakened.

'Yes, I want to know,' he said.

'Right,' she said, 'though I'm going to need some coffee myself first.'

He watched her make it, spending the time drinking his own coffee and trying not to think of how she looked naked; trying not to remember the sounds she made when she came.

It was a relief when she finally started talking, though he was still glad they had a breakfast bar between them.

'My mother was first diagnosed with ovarian cancer when I was seventeen, in my last year at high school. She was already stage four and the prognosis wasn't good. She still fought it, of course. Endured heaps of chemo. Her hair fell out and her weight dropped from sixty kilos to forty.'

'Good God. Poor woman.'

'Yes,' Ruby said bleakly.

'Your father must have been devastated.'

'He pretended to be. But the whole time she was dying, he was having an affair.'

'You're kidding me.'

'I kid you not. Mum wasn't cold in her grave before he took off to live with his other woman. She was rich, you see. A rich divorcee. Dad always wanted to be rich.'

Sebastian could hardly believe what he was hearing.

'Did your mother know?' he asked.

'I think she must have because she asked me to look after my brothers before she died. She didn't ask Dad.'

'So you stayed and looked after them.'

'Yes. I stayed,' she said in the kind of flat voice that hid a lot of emotion. 'Dad let us live in the house. He also paid the bills but I refused to take more of his rotten money than I had to. I worked part-time at the local fast-food place so I could buy my clothes and have some money in my purse.'

Sebastian's heart went out to the poor brave girl whose father had to have been the biggest bastard he'd ever heard of. 'What did your father do for a living?' he asked.

'He was a car salesman. Classic cars, actually. I think that's how he met the rich woman he took off with.'

'Didn't he come back home at all to see how you were faring?'

'Yes. Twice. But on the second occasion I told him what I thought of him and said I didn't want to see him again as long as I live. I meant it and he believed me.'

Sebastian didn't doubt it. Ruby was the type of girl

who meant what she said. 'And your brothers? What did they say about not seeing their father any more?'

'They were actually at school at the time of Dad's visit but when they came home, I told them what I'd said and they agreed with me entirely.'

'Both your brothers felt the same way?'

'Yes. They'd totally lost respect for Dad. We all had.'

'And have any of you seen your father since?'

'Not to talk to. I did email him once to tell him Liam and Oliver had graduated from university, and his response was to put the house on the market. He didn't bother to come to their graduation ceremony or buy them anything, not even a card.'

'Good grief. The man just gets worse and worse.'

'Indeed. Thankfully, Liam and Oliver had secured good jobs by the time the house was sold and could afford to rent. The real estate agent said they could take whatever furniture they wanted from the house once it was sold, which I presume Dad sanctioned.'

'How kind of him,' Sebastian said caustically.

'My thoughts exactly. Anyway, once the boys were settled, I took off. I'd had enough.'

'I can understand that. All those years raising your brothers was a lot of responsibility for a young girl.'

'It was tough,' she agreed. 'Dad's betrayal made me so angry. My boyfriend dumping me a year after Mum died didn't help, either. Bailey said I didn't have enough time to be a proper girlfriend. He complained I was always doing things for my brothers. Which was true, I suppose,' she added, sighing. 'Whilst they were loving boys, they could be selfish. And I guess I overcompensated a bit because of Mum dying and Dad deserting us. Still, if Bailey had truly loved me like he said he did, he would have helped me, not dumped me.'

'He certainly should have. When Jennifer was diagnosed, I tried to help. I offered to leave work and nurse her at home but she didn't want me to. She put herself into palliative care in hospital and stayed there until she died.'

'But what about her parents? Surely they would have offered to help care for her.'

'Her parents were both dead. They were killed in a car accident when she was a teenager. Jennifer was raised by her grandparents. By the time she got cancer, they had passed away.'

'I see. It sounds like there were no brothers or sisters either.'

'No. She was an only child. The circumstances of her upbringing made her very self-sufficient. She didn't like to need anyone. She was so damned tough at times. She told me once that she hadn't wanted to fall in love with me. She confessed she was afraid of losing me. Yet in the end it was me who lost her.' Sebastian's heart squeezed tight as he shook his head from side to side.

'What kind of cancer did she have?'

Sebastian's normal practice would be to stop talking about Jennifer as soon as possible but he couldn't seem to. 'Inoperable brain cancer. It came from a melanoma. She died within weeks of her diagnosis.'

'That's so sad.'

'People said it was a mercy she died so quickly but I couldn't handle it. It was all too sudden.'

'I can understand that. You didn't have time to get used to the idea of her dying.'

Was that why he'd fallen apart afterwards? he wondered.

Only partly, he accepted.

'Mum and I had two years to get used to her dying,' Ruby said. 'I valued that time I had with her. We became very close.'

'I envy you. Jennifer didn't want me to see her suffer, so she pushed me away. Every time I visited her in hospital she would tell me not to come again. I felt so helpless. Helpless and hopeless.'

'That was wrong of her,' Ruby said gently and Sebastian struggled not to cry.

'But that's no excuse for you not having her photos around,' she went on, less gently.

'That's a matter of opinion,' he said gruffly. 'People handle things differently, Ruby. I suggest we change the subject. It's going to be hot again today. How about coming for a swim with me later?'

'Am I allowed to wear my bikini?' she said cheekily.

'Absolutely not. That bikini is the work of the devil. That's what started me off on the road to ruin and damnation, seeing you in that bikini. So no, Ruby, I don't want you to wear that bikini. I don't want you to wear anything at all,' he finished up, smiling the sexiest smile.

CHAPTER EIGHTEEN

RUBY DID HER best to stay cool in the face of the wickedest of temptations, knowing instinctively that if she kept on giving in to this man, she would lose control of her life, and her emotions. She really didn't want to fall in love with Sebastian any more than he wanted her to fall in love with him. He didn't seem to appreciate the danger, however. But *she* did. It was bad enough that they'd started sharing confidences about their lives. Already she felt sorry for him. Already she wanted to somehow fix him.

Compassion and passion were a dangerous mix. Or they were where her soft heart was concerned.

'Sorry, Sebastian,' she said without a hint of the rampant desire raging within her. 'I have plans for today. First I have to do some Christmas shopping this morning. Then I have some studying to do this afternoon. I have an assignment coming up.'

'Can't you at least spare me a couple of hours? Surely you'll need a break from studying at some stage.'

'No. When I study I need total concentration. Going

skinny dipping with you would certainly break that concentration, as you very well know.'

'Fair enough. But I can't stand the thought of today without spending some time with you. So how about I go shopping with you?'

'You want to go shopping with me?' she asked, stunned. 'What if someone sees us together?'

'Like who? Gloria's in Adelaide and my mother never goes shopping on a Sunday. No one else matters.'

'I don't know about this, Sebastian,' she said worriedly. It was a strangely intimate thing, to go shopping together. Almost as bad as sharing confidences about your past life.

'I'll buy you lunch out,' he tempted, coming around to pull her into his arms.

She gasped at the feel of his near nakedness pressed against her, her heart racing as desire threatened to overwhelm her. His mouth sought hers and it was so exciting, his kiss, his nearness.

The sound of the house phone ringing startled both of them. Ruby reefed out of Sebastian's arms and snatched it up, glad of the distraction. If the kissing had gone on much longer, she'd have been back in bed with him. And she really didn't want to be that weak.

'It's your mother,' she told Sebastian as she put the phone to her ear.

'Good morning, Frieda,' she said breezily. 'How are you this morning?'

'Very well thank you, Ruby,' she returned, her voice not at all fragile. 'I just wanted to call and thank you for last night. It was a wonderful dinner. You are a wonderful girl. I hope Sebastian appreciates you.'

'I'm sure he does, Frieda,' she said, a naughty smile itching to break out.

'You'd make some man a wonderful wife.'

'You think so?'

'I do indeed.'

'That's very nice of you to say so. I'm afraid I have to go, Frieda. I'm in the middle of making your son's breakfast,' she lied.

'He's a fool, my son,' she muttered and Ruby pretended not to hear.

'What was that, Frieda?'

'Nothing. You go, my dear. Thank you again.' And she clicked off.

'Your mother thinks I would make some man a wonderful wife,' she murmured when Sebastian drew her back into his embrace.

That stopped him in his tracks. 'I'm sure she does,' he bit out. 'Why do you think I want to keep us a secret?'

'She just wants you to be happy, Sebastian. Mothers are like that.'

'Marriage is not necessarily the recipe for happiness. You should have told her you don't want to get married either.'

'Perhaps I should have. Now, I have to get us some breakfast,' she said, pulling out of his arms. 'Time is a-wasting. I'd like to get to the shops before they close.'

An hour passed before they were both properly fed and dressed, Sebastian continually delaying proceedings by kissing Ruby. He couldn't seem to keep his hands off her. Finally, they made it into his car and out to a nearby mall. The place was already packed, yet it was well off lunchtime.

'I'm not familiar with this mall,' Ruby said. 'Is there a department store or just smaller shops and super-markets?'

'There's definitely a department store. Come on. I know the way.'

When he took her hand in his, Ruby ground to a halt.

'No hand-holding in public,' she said firmly.

'Fair enough,' he replied. 'But I reserve the right to buy you lunch.'

'Okay,' she agreed. 'Shopping first, though.'

'Do you have anything specific in mind you want to buy?'

'Yes. I thought since both my brothers are in live-in relationships, I'd get them some seriously nice sheets and towels. At this time of the year, there are often sales in Manchester.'

'Sounds like a good idea,' Sebastian said.

Ruby couldn't believe how much she enjoyed the next hour. Sebastian was a great help, stopping her from buying navy blue sheets—despite them being a bargain—and insisting she stick to white, both with the sheets and the towels.

'Can't go wrong with white,' he advised.

As they made their way to the car park to deposit all their parcels before having lunch, it occurred to Ruby just how lonely she'd been for a long time. Yes, she'd made friends over the last few years, but they hadn't been close friends, and she'd moved too often to develop deep connections. Sebastian was the first person she'd gone shopping with in ages. And it had been so nice to have someone with her whose opinion she could ask.

Ruby suddenly thought of her mother and how they had always gone shopping together. For food. For clothes. Make-up. Anything and everything. Her father used to complain they were joined at the hip.

Thinking of her father annoyed her, so she shifted her mind to her brothers, who had always brought her joy. But they had their own lives now. She couldn't rely on them to ease her loneliness.

She couldn't rely on Sebastian either, she accepted ruefully. Once Georgia returned, she would be gone, from his life and his bed. She sighed before she could stop herself.

'What on earth are you thinking about?' Sebastian asked.

'Nothing important,' she replied, and dredged up a quick smile.

He frowned at her, then shrugged. 'Okay. I won't pry. You have a right to your thoughts. Are you hungry?' he asked as he zapped open the car. 'I am.'

'Not overly. But coffee would be nice.'

After they finished their coffee, they were making their way past some shops when Sebastian ground to a halt.

'That would be perfect for you,' he said, and pointed to a mannequin in a nearby window wearing a red dress.

It was, indeed, a stunning dress. Halter-necked, with a wide band inset around the waist above a gathered skirt—very short gathered skirt.

'That has Christmas party written all over it,' Sebastian said.

'No way could I wear a dress like that to your Christmas party,' Ruby protested.

'Nonsense. Let's go and try it on,' he said and this time firmly took her hand in his, pulling her into the expensive boutique.

When an attractive young salesgirl immediately approached them, a speechless Ruby let Sebastian do the talking.

'That red dress in the window,' he said. 'Ruby wants to try it on.'

'Certainly, sir,' the girl said happily and hurried away to find one in Ruby's size.

'It looks expensive,' Ruby whispered to Sebastian. 'This whole shop looks expensive.'

'Good. You only get what you pay for, Ruby. Now, no more objections. I'll be doing the paying. Call it a thank you for what you did for my mother's birthday.'

The dress was soon brought to them and Ruby was bundled off to try it on. It fitted perfectly, and looked very sexy on her. Sebastian obviously thought so too when she came out of the fitting room to show him. Desire flooded her as his eyes roved hotly over her. Suddenly, she couldn't wait to go home.

'Perfect,' he said. 'We'll take it.'

Ruby refrained from telling Sebastian that it cost almost a thousand dollars because he was right. He could afford it. And she loved the dress. It was gorgeous.

The salesgirl returned to the fitting room with her.

'You're a lucky girl, having a generous husband like that.'

Something twisted in Ruby's heart. 'He's not my husband,' she said.

'Oh, sorry. Boyfriend, then?'

'Something like that,' Ruby agreed, and smiled at the girl. For how could she say that he wasn't her boyfriend either, that he was her boss and her secret lover?

The girl left with the dress whilst Ruby got changed in her other clothes. She took her time, combing her hair whilst her mind whirled with bothersome thoughts. By the time she emerged from the fitting room, Sebastian had paid for the dress and had the parcel in his hand.

As they left the shop, Ruby decided to say what was on her mind. 'Thank you for the lovely dress, Sebastian, but I can't possibly wear it to your Christmas party. I'm your housekeeper, not a hostess.'

His sigh was full of exasperation as he stopped walking and turned to face her. 'At my annual Christmas party, you are neither, Ruby. This is a staff party and you are a member of my staff. Georgia used to get dressed up. Why shouldn't you?'

'Oh, I didn't realise.'

'No more objections, then?'

'I guess not.'

'Good, because I would like to get you home. Seeing you in that dress has done wicked things to me. I trust you won't come up with any other excuses not to spend some private time with me.'

He didn't wait for her answer, just headed for the car.

CHAPTER NINETEEN

THE DRIVE HOME was agony for Sebastian. He wanted Ruby so badly it was painful. As soon as he'd driven into the garage and switched off the engine, he turned and kissed her. It was possibly a mistake but he couldn't resist. He did stop, however, when disaster loomed. Lord, but she made him act like a randy teenager.

'I think I'd better get you inside, pronto,' he said wryly.

'Yes, please,' she said in a voice thickened with desire.

They only just made it up to his bedroom before they ripped each other's clothes off and fell onto the bed. Once again, their first mating was quick and savage, testimony to their need for each other. Afterwards, he carried her into the shower where they kissed under the water for ages till they were both panting with renewed need.

'I want you to put on that red dress for me,' he said as he dried her. 'Without any underwear, of course.'

He could see the idea excited her as much as it excited him.

She gave him one of those glazed looks, her chest rising and falling as her heartbeat quickened.

'I can't wear a bra with it anyway,' she said breathlessly.

'Yes. I noticed.' He still hadn't forgotten how she'd looked back in the shop. So hot and sexy that he'd immediately become erect.

'Will you take me with the dress on?' she choked out.

'Do you want me to?'

'Yes…'

So he did, getting her to kneel at the foot of the bed with her head on the quilt whilst he lifted the skirt and took her from behind. She moaned when she came, a noise of sheer pleasure. His own orgasm was just as intense.

'You are definitely trying to corrupt me,' she said when he pulled her shakily to her feet.

'I think the corruption is mutual. Now, take the dress off.'

Her inward breath could have been shock, but it felt more like excitement. She was one sexy woman.

Her hands trembled as she undid the side zip before slowly lifting the dress over her head, leaving her standing there once again with nothing on. Her breathing, he noted, had quickened further. His own was decidedly ragged.

'Take your hair down,' he ordered thickly.

Sebastian's gut tightened as she did so. God, but she was beautiful!

'You would tempt a saint,' he muttered.

She laughed. She actually laughed. 'But you're not a saint, Sebastian.'

'No,' he agreed. 'Far from it. Now stay where you are. There's something I have to do.'

He turned from the provocative sight of her nakedness, hurrying into the bathroom where he disposed of the used condom before rolling on another. The fact he was still so erect was as stunning as it was thrilling. He simply could not get enough of this woman. Thankfully, she seemed just as needy for him. He strode back into the bedroom where he climbed onto the bed, dragging in a few gathering breaths whilst he tried not to ogle Ruby too much. But he was wasting his breath. He couldn't stop looking at her. And wanting her.

'What do you want me to do?' she asked shakily.

'Nothing,' he growled. 'Just get that gorgeous body of yours over here.'

She came over to the bed rather hesitantly, which surprised him. Surely she wasn't going all shy on him. But no, she wasn't shy, he soon realised. She was trembling with desire.

'Wow,' she said, reaching out to brush her fingers over his erection. 'That's impressive, considering.'

Now it was his turn to laugh. 'It's been like this ever since I clapped eyes on you in that bikini, Ruby.'

Her eyes clouded and Sebastian worried momentarily that he'd said something to offend her. But then she smiled, and without any hesitation boldly climbed on top of him. Sebastian blinked his surprise. She hadn't taken the initiative before. He'd been the boss in the sex department so far, but he liked her taking charge.

'I could say the same when I saw you by the pool in those indecently tight togs you own,' she said, lifting her hips before taking a firm hold of his erection. Her eyes grew heavy as she eased him inside her, Sebastian unable to stop himself from groaning. Lord, but she was hot. Hot and wet.

'I didn't like you much to begin with, Sebastian,' she said as she began to ride him. 'But I always liked your body. You are one hunky man.'

Sebastian grimaced at her words, not happy that she'd reduced him to just a body. But he was too far gone to protest. He was close to coming, and so was she. He could recognise the signs. Her muscles tightened around him and her head tipped back, her lips parting as she dragged in more air.

He came first, shuddering into her as if he hadn't had an orgasm for years. She followed him with a fierce orgasm of her own, her hands clawing at his shoulders as she kept riding him through it, her eyes closed tight, till finally she stopped. For a long time she just sat on him, her eyes still shut. When she finally opened them, he was staggered to see they were wet with tears.

'What is it?' he asked straight away. 'What's wrong?'

She just shook her head and rolled off him onto the bed, her hands coming up to cover her face as she continued to shake her head from side to side.

Her tears upset him, for tears spelt emotion and emotion was something he'd vowed to avoid. Then again, he'd vowed to avoid sleeping with women like Ruby as well. But, hell on earth, he was only human and she was so incredibly sexy. Unfortunately, she was also an incredibly nice girl. He hoped she wasn't falling for him. If she was, then this affair was over. Pronto.

'You have to talk to me,' he insisted. 'Tell me what the matter is.'

She didn't reply, just sighed the deepest sigh.

Finally, she took her hands away, and Sebastian was relieved to see she wasn't still crying. Though her eyes were a little moist. She blinked as she turned to face him.

'It's nothing drastic, really. I was just overcome by the moment, that's all. I mean, I've never enjoyed sex like I enjoy it with you. It's incredible.'

Sebastian's relief was enormous. She wasn't falling in love with him. Thank God.

'You're the one who's incredible,' he said, and reached to cuddle to her close. 'Incredible all round. And the very best lover a man could have. You are insatiable, woman, and it's fantastic!'

'I guess I can't get used to having gone so sex mad. I mean, till I met you I was quite happy to be celibate.'

'Well, obviously that's not the case any longer. Face the facts, Ruby. You're a grown woman in her sexual prime. By your own admission it's been some time since you've had sex. It was inevitable that one day you'd meet a man who would turn you on. I myself have been on sexual rations for years so it's not surprising I had to break, eventually. Yes, we've both gone a bit sex mad but we're not hurting anyone. There's nothing wrong in what we've been doing. Yes, the arrangement I proposed is unconventional, but if it fulfils our needs at the moment, then why should we care, or worry?'

He tipped her face up and kissed her softly on her lips. 'Now, what say I order us a meal? I'm famished.'

'I am too,' she agreed.

'Okay, we'd better get dressed before the food arrives.'

'All right.'

'Then after we've eaten we'll come back upstairs to bed for the night.'

'Really?'

'Yes, really.'

'I would have thought you'd be too tired.'

'The food will revive me. But if we get tired, we'll go to sleep.'

'Am I to stay the whole night with you? Is that part of our arrangement?'

'I'd like you to.'

'We'll see,' she said. But she was smiling.

CHAPTER TWENTY

'How did Saturday night go?' was Janice's first question when she arrived on Monday morning.

'What are you talking about?' Ruby answered, alarmed that Janice somehow knew something.

'The dinner with the boss's mother,' Janice went on, giving Ruby a puzzled look. 'You can't have forgotten.'

She had, of course. The dinner for Sebastian's mother seemed like eons ago. All Ruby could think of this morning was what had happened on Saturday night. And last night. And then again this morning, after Sebastian awoke. The man was insatiable. But then, so was she. Already she could not wait for him to come home tonight and he'd only been gone a couple of hours.

'Oh, the dinner,' she said, hoping she didn't look as distracted as she was feeling. 'It went well.'

'I'll bet she liked the pie. My kids certainly did.'

'Yes, she liked everything,' Ruby said, only then noticing that Janice looked tired, which was understandable. The woman had three school-age children and a husband who Tom said was often out of work.

To earn money she worked hard as a cleaner, doing Sebastian's house, and Gloria's, as well as her own place.

'Come and have some coffee before you start,' she offered.

Janice glanced around her agitatedly. 'I should get on with things. The end-of-year presentation at the school is this afternoon and I promised the kids I'd be there. It starts at one-thirty.'

'You should be well and truly finished in time,' Ruby said. 'I'll help you.'

'Would you?'

'Of course.'

'You're a life-saver, Ruby. I... I want to go home and freshen up before I go. Do my hair. Put on a dress. The kids love it when I make an effort to look nice.'

'I'll make sure you're out of here in plenty of time.'

After their coffee, Ruby suggested Janice do the downstairs whilst she did the upstairs, leaving Ruby alone with her thoughts as she cleaned away. She started in the master suite, doing her best not to look at the bed and think about what had transpired there.

In truth, Ruby still hadn't come to terms with her bold behaviour, despite Sebastian's logical argument that they weren't doing anything wrong; that they were just indulging themselves sexually after denying themselves for too long.

It all sounded rational, but something inside Ruby kept ringing alarm bells. It was probably still just lust with both of them, but she wanted to keep it that way. Ruby didn't want to fall in love with her boss. She really didn't.

But such emotions didn't always respond to reason.

Eleven o'clock saw her come downstairs to tell Janice that she was finished upstairs, and if she wanted to go home early, she could.

'But I haven't done the bathroom down here,' Janice protested. 'Or got the laundry ready.'

'I'll do them. You go and make yourself beautiful for your children.'

Janice laughed. 'I'll do my best but I'd need a fairy godmother to look beautiful. I'll settle for nice.'

'Nonsense. You're a good-looking woman. Your husband is a lucky man.'

Janice's flush of pleasure gave Ruby pleasure. She liked making people feel good about themselves.

'He doesn't always think so,' Janice grumbled.

'Then he's a fool! Now off you go. I'll see you on Friday and you can tell me all about the presentation.'

'I'll do that,' Janice said cheerfully as she pulled off her cleaning gloves. 'Thank you so much, Ruby. You're a doll.'

Being called a doll brought a smile to Ruby's face. But once Janice had gone, it occurred to her that she was exactly that to Sebastian. A doll, to be played with for a while but easily discarded.

It was a depressing thought. But not, Ruby accepted ruefully, depressing enough to dampen her desire for Sebastian. She still wanted him to hurry home, still wanted tonight to come sooner than it would. She wanted him to take all her clothes off and, yes, to play with her at length before having all sorts of sex with her. There wasn't a position they'd tried that she hadn't enjoyed. She had no preferences as long as it was Sebastian she was having sex with.

Ruby sucked in sharply at this last revealing thought. Oh, dear. Maybe it was already too late. Maybe she was already emotionally involved with him. Not that it would change things. She was in way too deep to walk away. Just thinking about Sebastian made her fizz with longing. It didn't matter whether it was lust or love driving her actions. Until Georgia came back, she was his for the taking.

Strangely enough, the notion that she might be falling in love with Sebastian didn't upset Ruby as much as she'd thought it might. At least it showed she *could* fall in love. Ever since her father's betrayal, Bailey's cruel dumping, and Jason turning out to be married, she hadn't thought she would ever fall in love with a man. Or trust one, for that matter. Not that she needed to trust Sebastian. Such thinking was only an issue if he loved her back. Which he didn't. They didn't have a relationship. They had an *arrangement*, and it would come to an end in a few months.

Ruby was wondering how she would survive that when her phone rang, her chest tightening when she saw it was Sebastian.·

'Yes, Sebastian?' she answered, trying to sound like a housekeeper and not a woman obsessed.

'I have a problem,' he announced baldly. 'Those bastards I sold my shows to in the UK are trying to pull a swiftie with the contract and I have to go and sort it out. I've already booked a seat on a flight to London tonight but I need you to pack a bag for me and taxi it over to my office. I can't afford the time to come home and do it myself. I have things I have to do here before I go.'

'Can't this problem be fixed up over the Internet?' she said, dying inside at the thought she would not see him tonight after all.

'No. It needs my personal attention.'

'You haven't got a lawyer over there who could sort it out for you?'

'Afraid not. I'm the one and only lawyer I employ.'

'You're a *lawyer*?'

'That's what I was before I went into the television business. Jennifer was a lawyer too. That's how we met.'

'Oh. I didn't know.'

'Why would you?'

Yes, why would you, Ruby? It's not as though you two have ever really talked. You just have lots of sex.

But not tonight. Tonight, Sebastian would be winging his way to London, not to come back for possibly days.

'Don't forget your Christmas party is on Friday night,' she reminded him.

'I'll be back by then. I've booked a return flight that gets in Friday morning.'

'I see.'

'I'm sorry, Ruby,' he said quietly, and her heart turned over. 'I'll only be there a couple of days.'

'You'll be tired for your party.'

'I shouldn't be. I fly first class. I'll sleep on the plane.'

Ruby made no comment to this, having forgotten how super rich he was.

'I could bring your luggage to the airport,' she suggested hopefully. 'See you off.'

'Best not, Ruby. Just send the case to the office.'

'I don't know where that is,' she said, highlighting again how little she knew about this man.

He told her the address and she wrote it down.

'Before you go, Sebastian,' she said before he could hang up on her, 'would you mind if I had Tom put up some lights for the party? I mean, it's not a Christmas party without some Christmas decorations.' There were heaps in the storage room downstairs, obviously left behind by the previous owners.

His sigh down the phone was exasperated. 'You must know by now, Ruby, that I'm not into that kind of thing.'

'Yes, but—'

'Some lights, then,' he agreed abruptly before she could argue with him. 'But not out the front of the house. And no tree.'

'No tree?' she echoed.

'No tree,' he confirmed. 'Okay?'

'Okay.' But, boy, was she going to go to town on those lights.

'I'm sorry, I have to get back to work and you have to get on with packing me a bag.'

'Promise to text me tomorrow to let me know you've arrived safely.'

'For pity's sake, Ruby, this is just what I don't want.'

'All I'm asking for is a simple text,' she said firmly.

Another sigh. 'All right. I'll text you.'

'Thanks,' she said, but he was already gone.

Ruby trudged upstairs, trying to take some comfort from the fact that she knew so little about Sebastian. Because surely she couldn't be in love with a man she didn't know. It was just lust, she decided. Lust and infatuation. He was, after all, handsome and rich and, yes, damned good in bed.

Ruby brightened at this last thought, promising herself that when Sebastian arrived home Friday she would give him a welcome he wouldn't forget in a hurry.

CHAPTER TWENTY-ONE

SEBASTIAN'S PLANE TOUCHED down at Mascot shortly after seven on the Friday morning. Despite having flown first class, he was not rested, sleep having eluded him in London *and* during the long flight.

Sebastian's body sagged like a dead weight as he hauled himself out of his seat. His eyes felt gritty, his head full of cotton wool. Getting through Customs was slow and Sebastian had lots of time to regret having driven his car to the airport Monday. He should have left it at work and taken a taxi. He hadn't anticipated being this exhausted. Unfortunately, now he'd have to drive home instead of just sitting in the back seat of a taxi with his eyes blessedly shut.

Sebastian wasn't looking forward to the drive, or the arrival at home. He suspected by the time he got to the house he wouldn't be fit for much, certainly not the serious discussion with Ruby he'd decided upon during the long hours he'd been awake on the plane. Sebastian was not a procrastinator, but common sense demanded he put this off until he'd had some sleep. Such a situation needed tact and sensitivity. Not Sebastian's strong points. Especially not when he was exhausted.

The traffic home was appalling, peak hour on a Friday enough to try anyone's patience, let alone a man who hadn't slept properly in days. By the time he turned into his street at Mosman, he was practically comatose. Leaving his luggage in the car, he staggered up the stairwell. Ruby was in the kitchen, clearly eager for him to arrive if the smile on her face was anything to go by. That smile precisely underlined why he'd come to the decision he had.

'You're home!' she exclaimed happily. 'Can I get you some coffee? Some food perhaps?'

'Sorry,' he said far too sharply. 'But I don't want coffee right now. Or food, or anything else. I have to go to bed if I'm to function at the Christmas party tonight. No noise for a few hours, Ruby. We'll have coffee together later, when I feel human.'

It killed Sebastian to see the welcoming smile wiped off her face but it had to be done. He was being cruel to be kind, wasn't he? She'd see that he was right in the end.

Turning, he strode off down the hallway, hating himself more than he had in a long time.

Ruby stared after Sebastian until he disappeared. She heard him trudge upstairs and bang his bedroom door shut. Then she heard nothing.

She tried not to feel too hurt, tried to understand. Clearly, he hadn't slept on the plane. Clearly, the contract business he'd been going to fix in London had not gone well. But that was no reason to be so abrupt with her. It wasn't *her* fault.

Still, with Sebastian demanding no noise it was just

as well that Tom had done the lawns and pool yesterday. Just as well too that she'd given Janice the day
off, saying *she* would do whatever needed to be done.
Janice had been super grateful, as the school holidays
had begun and she wanted to spend more time with
her children. Of course, Ruby's motivation for doing
this wasn't all pure kindness. She'd been imagining
being alone in the house with Sebastian; she'd thought
that after a few days away he'd be as hungry for her
as she was for him.

Clearly not.

The erotically charged reunion Ruby had been fan-
tasising about all week was not going to happen, was
it?

Ruby tried to be philosophical about it. But it was
still disappointing. She'd been so looking forward to
being in Sebastian's arms again, to losing herself there
and feeling what he alone could make her feel.

She sighed deeply at the realisation that her feelings
had gone beyond lust now. Way beyond.

Oh, Lord. What to do?

Nothing, she accepted. She could do nothing. She
couldn't make Sebastian fall in love with her. He didn't
want that.

She could walk away, she supposed, before her
heart was totally broken. Maybe she should. She would
have to think about it. Ruby suspected, however, that
she simply didn't have the courage. Falling in love
made you weak. If she couldn't have Sebastian's heart,
she could at least have his body. For a while anyway.
Until Georgia got back.

Meanwhile…

Ruby wished she had some housework to do to distract herself but there wasn't any. The house was spotless, not a speck of dirt or dust anywhere. She supposed she could lie down and read a book, but, truly, what an anticlimax.

All the elation and anticipation Ruby had been feeling earlier had totally drained out of her. She'd been so looking forward to today. Not the party so much. Just Sebastian being back.

Okay, so he was tired, and obviously troubled. But that wasn't anything to do with her. He could at least have smiled at her, given her a little kiss maybe.

Perhaps she would just lie down and check out Facebook. See what those brothers of hers were up to. Yes, that was what she would do. That was how she'd kept in contact with them these past few years, though it was their female partners who posted most of the pictures.

Strangely enough, after she'd been doing that for a while her eyes grew heavy and before she knew it she fell asleep. She was awoken by the sound of the house phone ringing and Ruby was startled by the identity of her caller. It was Zack.

'Hi, Zack,' she said, trying not to sound too surprised. Or too worried. Surely he wasn't going to ask her out. She didn't want to have to tell him to get lost.

'Hi, Ruby. Look, I've been trying to get in contact with Sebastian but his damned phone's turned off. Is he there?'

'Yes, but he's asleep. He said he needed a few hours' rest before the party. I don't think he slept on the plane, and I have a feeling that contract business in London didn't go very well. He seemed worried.'

'Did he? Well, it's not about the business. That was all sorted out. Sebastian sent me a text. Look, he's probably just tired. Seb's not at his best when he's tired.'

'What did you want to contact him about? Maybe I can help. I wouldn't dare disturb him.'

'Okay. When he wakes up, tell him I might be a bit late for the party tonight. I will be there though. I promise.'

For such a laid-back kind of guy, Zack sounded somewhat stressed. Ruby couldn't let it go. 'Is there anything wrong, Zack?' she asked.

'Not really,' he said, still sounding odd. 'Just girl trouble. I wanted to ask Seb's advice about something. But no sweat, I'll sort it out myself. See you tonight.'

He hung up almost as abruptly as Sebastian did, leaving Ruby wondering what it was about men that they were compelled to be that way. Talkers, only occasionally. Confiders, rarely. Which was a shame because nothing good came of bottling up problems. If men shared more there would be less conflict between the sexes. Less mental illness as well.

Ruby glanced at the time on her phone. It was only one. There were still four hours to go before the caterers arrived, and at least three hours before she started getting herself ready for the party. She'd already decided not to go to town on her hair and face. Wearing that red dress was glamorous enough, so an hour would do. Rolling over, she picked up the novel she'd been trying to read all week, and started again at the beginning.

CHAPTER TWENTY-TWO

SEBASTIAN WAS ROUSED from his drugged sleep by a rather loud knocking on his bedroom door.

'What?' he said grumpily, his head still heavy from the sleeping pill.

'Sorry to disturb you,' Ruby said through the door. 'But it's gone seven o'clock and people will start arriving soon for the party. I thought you might want to be up and about to greet them.'

'Damn,' he muttered. 'Seven, did you say?'

'Actually, it's ten past.'

'Give me a few minutes and I'll be there,' he said, throwing off the quilt and lurching into the shower.

He started off with warm water, then turned it to cold, swearing under its icy spray until he was well and truly awake. He didn't bother to shave, just cleaned his teeth and combed his hair before heading to his walk-in wardrobe where he pulled on a pair of pale grey trousers, which were lightweight and cool. He teamed them with a favourite navy-blue shirt before slipping his feet into comfy black loafers and hurrying downstairs.

There were other people in the kitchen besides Ruby—a young man and a blonde girl—who were busily setting up glasses on the breakfast bar. But he only had eyes for Ruby, who was wearing that sexy red dress. Despite her hair being up with little make-up adorning her face, she still looked criminally desirable.

Damn, damn, and double damn!

'Hello, Mr Marshall,' the blonde girl said with a bright smile. 'I'm Marcie. We met last year, remember? And this is Josh, my partner in crime and catering.'

She and Josh both smiled at their in joke. Sebastian didn't smile back, troubled that the decision he'd come to on the plane was about to be swayed by the hunger Ruby instantly engendered in him. He told himself it wasn't Ruby herself he'd been missing, but the sex. He wasn't falling in love with her. There was no need to panic. No need to tell her their affair was over after all.

But down deep he knew he was kidding himself. He *was* in danger of falling in love with her. And he simply couldn't go down that road again. Not after what had happened with Jennifer.

'So how are you feeling now?' Marcie went on brightly, clearly undeterred by Sebastian's lack of humour. 'Ruby tells us you've just flown in from London and had to catch up on sleep.'

'I'm fine,' he said, thinking how typical it was of Ruby to chat away to these people as if they'd known each other for ever. Yet she would have only met this couple for the first time today. She was a very gregarious person. Gregarious and utterly gorgeous. Sebastian tried to keep his face impassive as he looked at her. Tried not to imagine reaching up and taking her hair down, then taking her to bed.

'I'll have coffee outside, Ruby,' he said, and spun away.

'Do you want anything to eat?' she called after him. 'You must be hungry.'

'We'll have lots of finger food ready shortly,' Marcie added.

'Just coffee for now,' Sebastian threw over his shoulder.

Ruby carried a mug of coffee out to where Sebastian was sitting at the outdoor table, glancing up at the lights. They were already turned on but wouldn't show to advantage until it got darker. She'd turned them on for a while last night and they'd looked fantastic.

Of course, old grumpy probably didn't like them. Truly, he'd try the patience of a saint at times. It pained her that she still found him so damned attractive, even when he was being a grouch. How she'd fallen in love with him she had no idea, though she suspected it had started the day he went shopping with her.

'The lights look good, don't they?' she said as she put the coffee down in front of him.

'Yes,' he surprised her by agreeing. 'They do, actually. But not as good as you.'

Ruby might have taken pleasure in his compliment if it hadn't been delivered so ruefully.

'Thank you,' she bit out.

'Would you sit down, Ruby? I need to talk to you about something before people get here.'

Ruby swallowed, knowing instinctively that she

wasn't going to like what he had to say. The hardness in his eyes rather gave the game away.

'Talk to me about what?' she asked tensely.

'Just sit down,' he bit out.

She sat down.

He sighed and shook his head at her.

'Well?' she prompted when he remained silent. 'What is it? People will be here soon. Or some of them will. And before I forget, Zack rang and said he'd be late. He tried to ring you but your phone was turned off.'

'Fine. Did he say why?'

'Some kind of girl trouble.'

'Of course.' His tone was dry, the implication being that Zack was always having girl trouble. It wasn't anything new.

'What did you want to talk to me about?' she went on when he didn't speak. He just sat there, drinking the coffee.

He finally put the mug down, pursing his lips before spearing her with a narrow-eyed gaze.

'I've had time to think whilst I was away,' he began firmly.

'About what?' she asked. But she had already suspected what was coming, her stomach flipping over before contracting tightly.

'Our arrangement,' he said. 'It's not going to work.'

'Why's that?' Ruby said, her chest tightening as well. 'I thought it was what you wanted.'

His laugh was cold. 'I thought so too.'

Ruby tried not to panic. Tried to keep calm. 'What *do* you want, Sebastian? Do you even know?'

'I know what I *don't* want,' he bit out. 'I don't want to fall in love again. The trouble is, you're the sort of girl a man falls in love with, especially once he starts sleeping with her.'

Ruby felt both flattered and frustrated. 'Is it so bad, falling in love again?' Quite the ironic statement, considering she'd once decided not to go there herself. But it was too late; she was already there.

'Yes,' he said firmly. 'I vowed not to fall in love again after Jennifer died and I mean to keep that vow. I'm sorry, Ruby, but I can't keep on—'

The front doorbell broke their conversation off at that critical point, leaving Ruby hanging. What had he been going to say? she agonised as he abruptly stood up and strode away. Clearly, she soon came to realise, she wouldn't be finding out until this party was over. People started pouring in, surprising Ruby that they'd turned up so early. She thought people were always late for parties these days.

Not this party, obviously. They all knew each other, which was logical. They all worked for Harvest Productions. She met so many new people during the next hour that she couldn't keep their names straight in her head. Still, she was glad she was wearing her lovely red dress because all the women were done up to the nines, some of them very beautiful and glamorous. They were all nice though, which came as a surprise. She'd thought they might all be up themselves but they weren't.

The DJ arrived and set up in the dining room from where the music could flow through the house and outside as well. The music he chose was a mixture of old and new, with some Christmas favourites thrown in occasionally. He was a big hit with the partygoers, if their dancing and singing along was any guide.

The lights were a big hit as well, several guests commenting on the festive spirit.

Ruby didn't feel very festive, despite having downed a few glasses of champagne as she chatted away to the guests. The alcohol didn't help her agitation at all. Or her depression. When Zack finally arrived, Ruby struggled to put a smile on her face. But she managed. Somehow.

'Hi,' she said after she opened the front door.

'Hi to you too,' Zack returned, giving her the once-over but without ogling. 'Wow, don't you look stunning? Red suits you.'

'And black suits you,' she said with her first real smile of the night.

'True.' He grinned. 'Sounds like the party's in full flow.'

He walked into the house—and the party—with his usual easy-going confidence, looking like a typical bad boy dressed all in black. Black jeans. Black T-shirt. Black belt and shoes. Even his tats were black. If she hadn't known he was a famous actor, Ruby would have thought he was a biker.

'Zack!' Sebastian exclaimed when he saw his friend. 'You made it.'

'Yeah,' he replied. 'Just. Did Ruby tell you I called earlier?'

'She did,' Sebastian replied with a swift glance her way. 'So what's up?'

'Nothing. Everything's sorted. What I need is a

drink. A *real* drink,' he added when a waiter approached with a tray full of champagne and wine.

'Come with me to the study,' Sebastian said, steering Zack away, leaving Ruby standing there staring after them. Annoyed, she swept another glass of champagne from the waiter's tray and lifted it to her lips, telling herself she really should eat something as well. It wouldn't be a good look for Sebastian's housekeeper to get drunk.

Such thinking had her heading for the kitchen, and the finger food. It was all delicious and very addictive. Ruby tasted just about every selection before heading back to the party, her heart lifting when she saw Zack and Sebastian had left the study, with Zack nursing a large whisky. Sebastian, however, surprised Ruby by choosing an orange juice from a passing waiter. He spotted her raised eyebrows and briefly raised his own, their eyes meeting across the room. It was a strangely intimate moment, one which could only happen between people who knew each other well.

Maybe she knew him better than she thought she did.

Wishful thinking, Ruby.

'Wow. Lights!' Zack exclaimed when he reached the al fresco area. 'That has to be Ruby's doing.'

'Of course,' Sebastian said with a rueful look her way. 'You don't think it was my idea, do you?'

Zack laughed. 'Never in a million years, mate. But they look great.' He turned to smile over at Ruby and she smiled back. Sebastian scowled at both of them.

The DJ packed up and went home at midnight, the party slowly breaking up after that. Most people had come in taxis and left the same way. Even Zack went home in a taxi, which was a good idea since he was plastered. No one asked to bunk down there for the night, highlighting their knowledge of their boss's passion for privacy.

The caterers were brilliantly efficient at putting everything away in the boxes in which they had brought everything, taking all the dirty plates and glasses with them when they left shortly after one. Ruby was very impressed and told them so as she helped them out to their van. There was nothing for her to do after they'd gone except turn the lights off and give the floors a quick going over with the vacuum cleaner. Out of the corner of her eye she saw two grey trouser legs appear.

'Ruby, stop with the vacuuming and come and sit down,' Sebastian commanded. 'We have to finish our conversation.'

Ruby sighed as she switched off the vacuum cleaner. 'I suppose we do,' she said, resigned to the inevitable.

'I'll be down in my study. See you shortly.'

Ruby put the vacuum cleaner away then trudged down to the study. Sebastian was sitting in the oversized leather chair in the far corner, the one with the standing lamp next to it. He was nursing a rather large whisky, which he lifted to his lips, his eyes spearing hers over the rim of the glass. He didn't look happy.

Ruby sat down in his office chair, her agitation spilling over when he remained silent.

'Well, out with it,' she demanded. 'What were you going to say earlier? Not that I don't already know.'

'What do you already know?'

'You don't want to sleep with me any more.'

'Actually, that's not true. I *do* want to sleep with you. That's the crux of the problem. What I was going to say earlier was that, under the circumstances, I can't keep you on as my housekeeper.'

Ruby's mouth dropped open as his words sank in.

'You're *firing* me?' she blurted out after a few mind-blowing seconds.

'I wouldn't put it that bluntly,' he ground out.

'And how would you put it?' she threw at him.

'I was going to suggest that you hand in your resignation, for which I would compensate you handsomely.'

Ruby couldn't help the disbelieving laugh that punched from her throat. 'You have to be joking. You're going to *pay* me to leave?'

'It seems only fair.'

Fair. Ruby closed her eyes against the crippling hurt in her heart.

'I'm sorry, Ruby,' he said with a weary sigh. 'But I can't see any other way. I never meant to hurt you. Or to interfere with your plans. But if you stay, things will get complicated.'

Complicated. That was putting it mildly.

'Very well,' she said at last. 'I'll go.' Best she did, really. 'But I don't want your damned money.'

'Don't be stupid,' he snapped as he stood up and walked towards her. 'You deserve compensation. It was wrong of me to do what I did, and to suggest such an arrangement in the first place.'

'I went into it with my eyes open,' she admitted ruefully.

'I suppose you did, but that doesn't make me feel

any better. Please, Ruby, let me make things comfortable for you, make that dream of becoming a social worker come true. I'm a rich man. I can afford to buy you an apartment. Or just give you cash, if you prefer.'

Ruby realised it probably would be stupid of her to refuse his offer. He was right. He was a rich man. A very rich man. Nevertheless, refuse it she would.

She stood up, her shoulders squaring as she faced him.

'I don't want you to buy me an apartment or give me a great wad of cash. As I said, I went into our affair with my eyes open. I wanted to sleep with you and I ignored the warnings in my head that nothing good ever comes of sleeping with the boss. I'll be gone in the morning. And don't worry, I won't be telling anyone the truth. I'll just say things didn't work out. I'll claim a personality clash. That's always a good reason to quit. But I will expect an excellent reference, plus *some* severance pay. A month's wages seems fair. Okay?' she said as she walked out from behind the desk.

Sebastian caught her before she could escape. 'I can't tell my mother or my sister that we had a personality clash. They won't believe me.'

'Well, that's too bad, Sebastian. You'll have to figure something out. Of course, you could try telling them the truth. That you asked me to leave because we've been sleeping together and you're suddenly scared stiff of becoming emotionally involved. That's the crux of the matter, isn't it?' she threw at him. 'Any kind of relationship is too risky for you, even a sexual one. You might actually start caring for me and vice versa. Shock horror!'

He looked quite crushed by her sarcasm, his hands dropping from her shoulders as his whole body sagged. 'Yes. That pretty much hits the nail on the head. I'm sorry, Ruby, but yes, you're spot on.'

Ruby should have walked out then and there but she couldn't. His expression grew so bleak. And so lonely. Before she could think better of it she reached up and gently touched the cheek of the man she loved.

'There's no reason why we can't enjoy each other one last time, is there?' she said, her fingers running a sensual trail down his face. 'Sort of a going-away present. For me.'

His eyes showed how tortured he felt. And how tempted. His hand came up to cover hers. 'Oh, God, Ruby,' he said with a groan. 'Don't.'

But it was too late. She was already lifting herself up on tiptoe and pressing her mouth to his.

CHAPTER TWENTY-THREE

No, NO, *NO*! Sebastian's head screamed at him when he started to kiss her back.

But it was too late, because his lower body was screaming *yes, yes, yes* much louder.

All common sense fled. Her lips enticed him, as did the hot blood roaring through his veins, flooding him with the need to give her what she wanted, what *he* wanted.

Oh, yes, he wanted it, desperately, his hands winding around her back and pulling her hard against him.

But it startled him when she wrenched backwards.

'No. Not here,' she said firmly. 'Come with me.'

She took his hand and led him from the study down the hallway and into her bedroom. There, she drew him over to the side of the bed where she started to undress him.

'Don't say a word,' she said, her voice cool but her dark eyes glittering wildly.

He complied, his tongue thick in his throat as she removed his shirt then his belt and then his trousers.

'Kick off your shoes,' she ordered, which he did, leaving him standing there in just his boxers.

When she hooked her fingers into their elastic waistband he noticed that her hands were trembling. Good, he thought.

Good? What was good about it? He didn't want her nervous. He wanted her wanton and wicked and without one shred of decency. He wanted to hate her for doing this to him.

When she pulled his boxers down he hoped she would go down on her knees before him. That way, it would be just sex with her. But she didn't. Instead, she stepped back and just stared at him, drinking in the sight of him. Not just his erection but his whole body. His face. His chest. His legs. She looked him up and down and sighed, giving him the weirdest feeling that she was trying to memorise him, which was crazy.

Her smile, when it came, was a relief. Because it was all those things he wanted her to be. Wanton and wicked, and, yes, sexy as hell.

She quickly disposed of her lovely red dress and the underwear she had on.

His own smile was just as wicked as hers as his eyes gobbled up every inch of her very beautiful body.

He pounced, making her squeal as he swept her up into his arms and threw her onto the bed.

His hands found all those places that his eyes had admired before moving on to places that couldn't be seen. She moaned beneath the onslaught of his passion. Or was it fury? Maybe a bit of both. Sebastian was beyond thought. Beyond reason. He no longer cared about the emotional risk attached to sleeping with Ruby. He no longer cared about anything but sinking inside her and satisfying the needs that had been tormenting him ever since he met her. She was the devil incarnate, he decided. Teasing him. Tempting him. But he would turn the tables on her tonight. He would not stop until she was begging him to. Once would not be enough. Ten times would not be enough. If she wanted a goodbye present, he would give her a night she would never forget.

Sebastian woke with a start, blinking as he tried to work out what had woken him. Then the sound came again. Muffled but familiar. His phone.

After a wry glance at Ruby, who was still dead to the world next to him, he leant over the side of the bed and retrieved the phone from his trouser pocket.

The identity of the caller eluded him. It was a private number not connected to his contacts menu. If it was a scam call, he wasn't going to be a happy man. Actually, he wasn't a happy man already, his resolve to reduce Ruby to begging not having worked out that way. They had both fallen asleep after that first torrid time, sleeping through until now. A glance at his phone showed it was five-twenty-four a.m. God. Almost dawn. Sebastian tried to blame exhaustion from his trip, followed by the party, but he suspected his age was catching up with him.

'Yes?' he said sharply into the phone, never giving his name to an unknown caller.

'Is that Mr Marshall? Mr Sebastian Marshall?'

It was a woman's voice. Australian. Brisk. Efficient.

'Yes,' he said.

'I'm calling from ER at St Vincent's hospital. We had a patient brought in in the early hours of this morning. Mr Zachary Stone. He's given us your name and number as his first line of contact. I did ring before but there was no answer.'

Sebastian ignored Ruby's hand on his arm, as well as her whispered *what is it*?

'What's happened to him?' he asked anxiously.

'He was stabbed in the stomach. By a crazy lady, according to the patient.'

'My God! Is he all right?'

'He's not on the critical list. And he was conscious when he came in. That's how I have your name and number. Anyway, he's just been taken up to surgery. I can't tell you any more right now, Mr Marshall, I'm sorry. I would suggest you come in, if you can. It's always good for a patient to see a familiar face when they wake up. Though you might have a bit of a wait.'

'That's all right. I'll be there as soon as I can. Thank you,' he added, but she'd already hung up.

'What is it?' Ruby demanded to know straight away. 'What's happened?'

'Zack's been stabbed. By some crazy lady, apparently. He's in hospital, being operated on right now. Look, I have to go.' He jumped out of bed and reached for his clothes.

'I'm coming with you,' she said, doing exactly the same.

'Don't be ridiculous. What will Zack think if you show up there with me at this hour?'

'I don't care what he thinks, Sebastian. I refuse to stay here, worrying myself sick.'

Sebastian hated the jealousy that flared at her words. 'And why would you worry yourself sick over

Zack? Is there something going on between you that I don't know about?'

'Oh, don't be so pathetic. He's a friend, that's all. I care about my friends, especially ones who need caring about. Can we stop with this useless bickering and get going?'

Twenty minutes later they zoomed into a space in the hospital car park, neither of them having spoken during the entire trip. Sebastian had been too worried about Zack to talk.

'What if he dies?' Ruby said as they climbed out of the car.

'He won't die,' Sebastian stated with more surety than he was feeling. 'Zack's as tough as an old boot.'

'Is he? I think he has a very soft underbelly.'

Sebastian stopped to stare at her. 'You have a highly intuitive nature, don't you?'

She frowned. 'What do you mean?'

'Most people look at Zack and think nothing can hurt him. But they'd be wrong.'

'Would you like to explain that?'

'No. I wouldn't.'

'Should we take flowers?'

Sebastian laughed. 'Hell, no. He'd be mortified.'

'Okay,' Ruby said, and smiled at him.

Her smile did things to Sebastian that worried him almost as much as Zack's condition. He suspected it was already too late to stop becoming emotionally involved with her. Maybe it wasn't love yet, but it was certainly more than just sex. He shouldn't have let her seduce him last night. It had been one time too many. Where would it all end?

Still, he had more to worry about at the moment than his own stupid self.

'Let's go,' he said, and headed for the lifts.

CHAPTER TWENTY-FOUR

RUBY SAT WITH Sebastian in the waiting room, having been informed that Zack was fine but still in recovery. They would be told when they could see him. Whilst they waited, Ruby got them both some coffee from the machine in the corner of the room, but it was pretty awful.

The wait seemed interminable, broken only by two policemen coming along to interview Sebastian. He told them he knew nothing about the attack, or the woman who'd attacked Zack. They would just have to wait to interview the man himself. The police did say that Zack had made no attempt to protect himself from the knife-wielding assailant, a witness stating that he had just stood there with his hands up and let the woman stab him in the stomach. Twice. Ruby found this news astonishing whereas Sebastian, she noted, didn't seem overly surprised.

Finally, after the policemen had interviewed Zack, they were let into the private room he'd been taken to. By this time it was the middle of Saturday morning.

'Not too long, mind,' an officious nurse named Susan informed them. 'Mr Stone needs his rest.'

Zack did look pale, lying back on a mountain of pillows with lots of tubes and machines connected to him. When they walked in, Zack glanced from Sebastian to Ruby then back to Sebastian, his eyebrows lifting a little.

'How are you feeling?' Sebastian asked, coming forward to place a gentle hand on Zack's forearm.

The gesture moved Ruby. So Sebastian could actually care for someone, could he? It gave her some kind of hope. Though not too much. She suspected he would still want her gone today, despite last night.

'The doctor said the surgery went well,' Zack told Sebastian. 'Isn't that right, Susan?' he directed to the nurse, who was hovering.

'As well as can be expected, Mr Stone.'

'Do call me Zack, please. They said I'd be in here for at least a week. Time for us to become best buddies.'

She blushed. She actually blushed. But her eyes flashed daggers at him.

'None of that, thank you, Mr Stone. Now, I'll be back when you need your catheter bag changing in a quarter of an hour. Until then, try to behave yourself and just rest.'

'Wow,' Sebastian said after she hurried away. 'You won't be winding that one around your little finger.'

Zack pulled a face. 'You could be right there.'

'Tell us about the woman who stabbed you.'

'Nothing to tell. I don't know her from Adam. She's an obsessed fan who's been stalking me for a while. She's been hanging around my building for weeks. Takes photos of me all the time.'

'Did you tell the police that?'

'I reported her to the local cops before I came to your party. That was what set her off—them going to speak to her. She pretended to go away but she didn't. She lay in wait for me till I came home from the party and ran at me, screaming, with a knife.'

'Which you made no attempt to stop.'

'No,' he said in a voice that puzzled Ruby. It was oddly resigned.

'You know why not,' he added sharply, looking straight at Sebastian. 'I couldn't risk it.'

Sebastian nodded. 'I understand.'

Maybe he did but Ruby sure as hell didn't.

'But, Zack—' she began, only to be cut dead by Sebastian's savage glare.

'Ruby wanted to bring you flowers,' he said, filling in the awkward moment.

'What kind of flowers?' Zack asked her.

'Not sure. Sebastian said you wouldn't like them.'

'Then he'd be wrong. I'd love flowers. Why don't you go and get me some? There's sure to be a florist here somewhere.'

Ruby was no fool. She knew Zack was getting rid of her so he could talk to Sebastian alone. Whilst somewhat annoyed, she still went in search of a florist, at the same time determined to find out answers to her questions as soon as possible. If Ruby had one flaw it was an insatiable curiosity about people. She wasn't a gossip but she just liked to *know*!

The florist was down a couple of floors. By the time Ruby returned with a basket full of multi-coloured blooms the nurse called Susan was back, glowering at Sebastian. She rolled her eyes at Ruby, taking the basket from her and placing it on a nearby windowsill.

'I'm sorry, but you'll have to go now,' she said firmly. 'Mr Stone is not long out of surgery and he needs his rest.'

'There's no arguing with that one,' Sebastian muttered as they left.

'She's just doing her job,' Ruby said. 'You can visit Zack again tomorrow. Take him some fruit and some chocolates.'

'Zack doesn't eat fruit. Or chocolates.'

Ruby was quite taken aback. What kind of person didn't eat fruit or chocolates?

'That's most unusual,' she said.

'Just habit. There was a time in his life when fruit and chocolates weren't large on his menu.'

'What time was that?'

'I'm not sure I should tell you. It's Zack's private business. I shouldn't have said anything.'

'Would you at least tell me why Zack didn't defend himself against some knife-wielding stalker? He's a fit, strong man. It doesn't make sense.'

Sebastian gave her a long look, which Ruby couldn't fathom. Something was going on in his head. Something serious and thought provoking. But what?

Clearly, he wasn't about to confide in her, since her question remained unanswered. And why *should* he confide in her? She was about to exit his life. It was a depressing thought, one that she'd managed to keep at bay whilst they'd been visiting Zack. But it had still been there, hovering.

'I'll tell you later,' he whispered unexpectedly as

they reached the lifts that would take them up to the level where the car was. 'When we're alone,' he added, nodding towards the group standing next to them.

Ruby was taken aback by this offer, but pleased too. As soon as they reached the privacy of Sebastian's car, she turned to him.

'Please don't start driving before you tell me why Zack did what he did.'

'Very well,' he agreed. 'But you must promise never to tell anyone.'

'I give you my solemn word.'

Sebastian nodded. 'Right. The thing is, Zack spent five years in jail. From the age of eighteen to twenty-three.'

Ruby could not have been more shocked. Zack might look a bad boy but she instinctively knew that he wasn't, not deep down. 'How on earth did that happen? I mean, what did he do?'

'He killed a man.'

'What?'

'It was an accident,' he insisted.

'Look, I believe you. What happened exactly?'

'Zack went up to the Cross to celebrate his eighteenth birthday. There was this guy who was drunk and abusing his girlfriend outside a club. He was calling her names, slapping her around. When Zack stepped in and asked him to stop, the guy started swinging punches. Zack fought back. The guy fell and hit his head. He died a week later.'

'But it was self-defence, and an accident,' Ruby argued, appalled. 'There had to have been witnesses. What about the girlfriend?'

'She turned on him, said it was all his fault. It also didn't help that he couldn't afford a good lawyer. Still, what does it matter now? It's too late to change anything. Zack was convicted of manslaughter. He got ten years, paroled in five.'

Ruby's heart went out to eighteen-year-old Zack. 'The poor boy.'

'You're absolutely right. He was just a boy at the time. He changed his name after he got out. Changed his appearance, too, by growing his hair. He'd had a buzz cut in jail. His mother helped him, shortly before she died.'

'He told me his mother died when he was young,' Ruby said, thinking back to the night they'd chatted together outside. He'd hinted at having a secret, but she would never have guessed this. 'How did she die?'

'She was hit by a cement truck as she crossed the road. It happened not long after he was released from jail.'

'How awful.'

'Yes, his mother was all he had. She'd been a single mum; his dad took off years before.'

'That's so sad.'

'Yes, it is. She's the one who also suggested Zack try out for modelling after he got out of jail and no one would give him a job. He took her advice, but not until after she died. Anyway, that led to him auditioning for acting jobs, and the rest, as they say, is history.'

'It's due to his mother, then, that he became a success.'

'Absolutely. She would have been so proud of him.'

'Maybe she still is,' Ruby said. 'Maybe she's looking down on him from heaven. Maybe she kept him safe last night.'

'That's a nice thought.'

Ruby didn't like to add that she often thought of her mother looking down on her from heaven. It was a comfort when she felt lonely. Though not so much when she was doing things she shouldn't be doing, like sleeping with her boss. And stupidly falling in love with him.

Her sigh was weary.

Sebastian sighed as well. 'At least now you can understand why Zack didn't defend himself last night.'

'He was afraid of somehow going back to jail again. That's so sad.'

'Yes, it is. But it's not a good way to live your life, being afraid,' he said thoughtfully. 'It's stultifying.'

His remark startled her. Then made her think. Was he still talking about Zack being afraid? Or himself?

'We all try to protect ourselves from hurt,' she said, well aware she'd spurned the opposite sex for years for that very reason. 'It's only natural.'

'Yes, but fear can get out of control. And when it does, it's self-destructive. Zack could have died tonight.'

'But he didn't.'

'No, because he was damned lucky.'

'I suppose so,' she said, not sure where this conversation was heading.

But it didn't head anywhere because Sebastian abruptly started the car and reversed out of the space. 'We'll talk some more when we get home,' he said brusquely. 'After I've had something to eat. I'm famished. I can't think when I'm starving.'

And that was that. Silence descended and Ruby was left up in the air.

CHAPTER TWENTY-FIVE

SEBASTIAN HAD LIED. He *could* think all right. In fact, that was all he did the whole way home. Think.

Zack's near brush with death had been a shock, but it had also woken Sebastian up to the way he was living his own life. In fear. Since Jennifer's death, he'd been afraid of falling in love again, afraid of giving away his heart and having it broken, either by death or divorce or some kind of disaster. He'd managed to survive so far by becoming a workaholic but, really, it was a nothing life. And a lonely life.

Ruby was right to call him pathetic, because he was. Any normal man would have been thrilled to have such a woman as Ruby come into his life. But what had he done? Run a mile to begin with, until he couldn't resist her any longer. And then what? He'd tried to control things by coming up with that ridiculous proposition.

She would surely pack up and leave today if he didn't stop her. So yes, he had to stop her.

Maybe not tell her he loved her. That would be a step too far at this stage. But he had to show her that he cared. And he had to offer her something better than a strictly sexual arrangement.

'I hope you're not expecting me to cook you breakfast before I leave?' she said tartly when he stopped the car outside the garage and waited for the door to rise.

'No,' he replied carefully.

'Good. Okay. When do you want me out by?'

He turned to her, his eyes determined. 'I don't want you to leave at all.'

Her own eyes widened. 'You don't?'

'No, I want you to stay.'

'But last night, you said…you said…'

'That was last night. Things have changed since then. Could we talk, Ruby? Really talk?'

He had rarely seen her so flummoxed. 'I… I guess so.'

'Good.'

In the end, she did cook him some breakfast. Nothing complicated—just French toast and coffee. They ate it outside on the terrace, Sebastian doing his best not to look as nervous as he was. He wasn't confident she would say yes to what he intended to propose. Ruby was strong-minded, not likely to be flattered or manipulated into what he wanted. She could very well tell him to get stuffed and still leave. It wasn't as though she were in love with him. She'd made it quite clear that she wasn't. Finally, when the toast was gone, he bit the bullet and spoke up.

'The thing is, Ruby. I care about you. It's not just the sex. I want you to stay. I want you to be my girlfriend.'

Ruby's heart stopped beating. 'Girlfriend?' she repeated, stunned by this totally unexpected announcement. When he'd been so dour during the drive home, she'd been sure it was all over; that she was to be out of the door that same day.

'Yes. Girlfriend,' he repeated, standing up and coming around the table to sit in the chair next to her. 'But only if you want to, of course.'

'Only if I want to…'

'Yes.'

Her joy was instant. But so was the temptation to tease him. 'Well, let me see now…'

When a sheepish smile spread across her face, he shook his head at her. But his blue eyes sparkled. 'You are a minx,' he said, reaching out to cup her face before leaning over and kissing her.

It was a gentle kiss. A loving kiss, nothing but lips. It surprised Ruby. Sebastian was usually a passionate kisser. But she liked the tenderness of his mouth, and his hands. Liked it a lot.

When his head lifted, he opened his mouth to say something, but then he closed it again and just shook his head at her.

'Don't take this the wrong way, Ruby,' he said at last, 'but I still want to keep our relationship a secret for a short while.'

'Our relationship?' she said, startled by his use of the word.

'Yes. Relationship,' he confirmed. 'A proper one. The trouble is, if we tell my family and friends that we're an item, they'll start interfering. I want to keep you to myself for a while at least, whilst we figure this out.'

Ruby didn't know what to say. She was thrilled

that he wanted her as his girlfriend, but wary over him wanting to keep it a secret, even for a short while.

His smile was reassuringly warm, however. Warm and quite sweet. 'You've made me break all my life rules,' he said. 'You know that, don't you?'

'You've made me break a few of mine as well,' she returned, his words slowly sinking in. Did she dare hope he might feel for her what she felt for him? Or was that too good to be true? He hadn't said he loved her, just that he cared for her. It wasn't the same.

'Sebastian,' she said when her wariness raised its ugly head again.

'Yes?'

'I understand why you would want to keep us a secret for a while, especially from your mother. But I don't want to spend Christmas Day with her, pretending to be just your housekeeper. I mean, for me, having a real relationship shouldn't be about pretending.'

'You're right,' he said. 'It shouldn't. We'll tell them all on Christmas Day that we're dating, okay?'

'Yes, all right,' she said, suddenly worried that they might think she'd taken advantage of her position to seduce Sebastian; that she was some kind of gold-digger.

'If it really bothers you, Ruby, I'll ring them up and tell them today.'

'No, no,' she said hurriedly. 'Please don't. Christmas Day will do fine.'

'Why are you frowning, then?'

'I don't know. I guess I… I'm worried your family might think badly of me.'

'Why on earth would they do that? My mother already loves you.'

Ruby sighed. 'I suppose you're right.'

'I am right,' he said, and gave her another kiss. 'So what are we going to do today, girlfriend?'

'Nothing much. I'm awfully tired.'

'In that case I think we should go back to bed. I might even let you go to sleep.'

'Thank you very much,' she said, giving him a peck on the lips. 'If you do, you might get a reward when I wake up.'

CHAPTER TWENTY-SIX

SEBASTIAN WAS REWARDED HANDSOMELY, pleased to finally make love to Ruby with true affection in his heart. The sex they'd been having had been physically exciting, but it was even better when it was an expression of love. Oh, yes, he'd finally come to terms with his feelings for Ruby. It was love that he felt for Ruby. True love. Deeper than he'd ever felt before.

He'd loved Jennifer, but it had been a young man's love. Passionate, yes. But selfish. Lacking in maturity and understanding.

He understood Ruby. Understood that she'd been hurt in the past, that she'd had her faith in men shattered. That father of hers had been appalling. Then, when she'd needed him the most, her boyfriend had dumped her. Sebastian suspected there'd been other creeps in her life as well.

It would take a while to win her trust and her heart. Yes, Ruby lusted after him. Maybe she even cared about him a little. But he doubted she loved him. And why would she? He'd hardly been all that loveable. But he aimed to pull out all the stops from this day forward. He wanted her to love him, wanted it more than he'd wanted anything in his life.

Sunday dawned fine and sunny, Ruby waking in Sebastian's bed, feeling wonderfully rested and sated. Sebastian's lovemaking had taken a tender turn the night before, but she didn't mind. She liked him taking his time, liked looking into his eyes and thinking how much she loved him. They'd snuggled up and talked for ages before falling asleep, Ruby happy to find out more about Sebastian—the man, not just Sebastian her boss and secret lover. He liked movies, which was a given, considering his profession. He liked reading. Liked swimming. She'd confessed to her own love of all three, which seemed to please Sebastian a lot.

Unfortunately, as she lay there the next morning, thinking about how much she loved the man lying next to her, Ruby's happiness slowly began to fade. She began worrying about what would happen when Georgia came back, when she was no longer conveniently living in his house. Did Sebastian plan to set her up in an apartment nearby and visit her on occasion?

He didn't know her very well if he thought she would go for such an arrangement.

When Sebastian started to stir, Ruby told herself to stop with the infernal thinking and worrying. *Enjoy what you have right now, you foolish girl. Because that's all you can be sure of in life, isn't it?*

'Did I tell you that Harvest Productions has closed down for the summer break?' Sebastian told her over breakfast.

'No,' she replied, reminding her that there was still a lot she didn't know about Sebastian.

'Yes. We do the same thing every year. It's better to have everyone off at the same time.'

'When do you go back to work?'

'The second week in January. Until then, the television channels run repeats. Or put something else on.'

'What about *Battle at the Bar*? When do you start shooting the next season?'

'Not till late January but it will depend on Zack. Hopefully, he'll be better by then. We'll know more when we visit him today.'

Ruby frowned. 'I was thinking about that. What if we run into other people from Harvest Productions at the hospital? They'll think it's odd if I'm with you. They might put two and two together.'

'I doubt we'll run into anyone. The story's not out about Zack being stabbed yet. I checked the news on my phone earlier and there was nothing.'

'But it won't take long to get out,' Ruby said. 'Someone will talk.'

'Not Zack. He's not into social media. Or media at all, for that matter.'

'What about the police? Or one of the nurses?'

'It's possible. Look, don't worry about running into other people at the hospital. It's none of their business if you're there with me.'

'I suppose so…'

'Come on. Let's get dressed and get in there. The earlier we visit, the less likely it will be that anyone else will be there.'

Sebastian was right. There was no one else in

Zack's room, other than the nurse named Susan who was checking his blood pressure. She glanced up as they entered, giving Ruby a look that wasn't entirely welcoming.

'You look a bit better than yesterday,' Sebastian remarked whilst Ruby sat down on a chair in the corner. 'But not much.'

'Don't worry, Seb. Susan says I'll be okay in a week or so. Isn't that right, Susan?'

'If you're sensible and do as you're told.'

'I can't really do anything else, can I? They won't even let me out of bed yet.'

'We'll be getting you out of bed later today,' Susan informed him briskly.

'Thank God for that.'

Ruby was glad when the nurse left the room so they could talk naturally.

'So how are you really feeling, Zack?' Ruby asked.

'Awful. But at least I'm alive. And that nutcase has been arrested.'

'Poor woman,' Ruby said. 'She's obviously mentally ill.'

'Probably. But she needs professional help.'

'Has anyone else been in to visit you yet?' Sebastian asked.

'No. You're it.'

'Do you want me to tell the others at work? I could send out a blanket email.'

'Not yet. Maybe in a day or two.'

'By then it'll probably hit the news and they'll know anyway.'

'Hopefully not. I asked the police to keep it quiet. And the hospital.'

Sebastian nodded. 'Good thinking.'

'From the sounds of things,' Ruby said, 'you definitely won't be out before Christmas. That's only four days away.'

'You're right there. The doctor says I'll be here for longer than that.'

'That's a shame,' Ruby said. 'But we'll come and visit you on Christmas Day. Bring you lots of presents.'

'Nah. None of that. We never exchange presents at Christmas, do we, Seb? But I tell you what.' He directed this at Sebastian. 'Bring me a couple of books from your rather extensive library. Thrillers, preferably. And soon. There's nothing on the TV at this time of year except cricket,' he said, pointing up to the TV mounted on the wall.

'Will do,' Sebastian said. 'I'll bring you a couple tomorrow.'

'Thanks.'

'I can't come tomorrow,' Ruby said. 'I have Janice and Tom coming, and lots of housekeeping things to do.'

'I'll still come,' Sebastian said just as nurse Susan hurried in.

Truly, did she have any other way of moving?

'I have to do Mr Stone's observations,' she informed them. 'I suggest you step outside for a minute.'

Ruby stood up and went with Sebastian into the corridor, having noted his face had gone a bit ashen.

'You all right?' she asked him.

'Yeah. I'm fine. Hospital procedures still get to me a bit. It's crazy, really.'

'No, not at all,' she said gently, and placed a soothing hand on his arm. 'Bad memories.'

He covered her hand with his and smiled at her. 'When we're finished here, Ruby, would you come shopping with me, help me buy my mother a few Christmas presents? Gloria and I don't exchange presents any more. And I always just give the boys money. But Mum likes her presents and I never know what to buy.'

Ruby smiled back at him. 'So what lucky lady usually does the honours for you?'

'My PA. Or Gloria. But I just know you'd be better at choosing. You get people, Ruby. You really do.'

Ruby felt her heart flutter with his compliment. 'I do my best.'

They had a lovely few hours during which Ruby found all sorts of interesting gifts for Frieda, the CBD having a wide range of shops. After they returned their parcels to the car, Sebastian suggested lunch. They found a place that wasn't too busy, both of them sitting down with slightly weary sighs.

When the waitress brought their order, conversation was suspended for a couple of minutes. Unfortunately, silence had a way of bringing Ruby's worries to the forefront of her mind. She wasn't a girl who liked to dwell endlessly on worries if she could talk about them, so once Sebastian had finished his meal she spoke up.

'Would you mind if I ask what you see happening once Georgia returns?'

Sebastian frowned, then picked up his coffee for a swallow before answering.

'I'm sure we'll have sorted something out by then,' he said.

Ruby frowned as well. 'That sounds rather vague. I like to know where I stand, Sebastian.'

'Yes, I can see that. But could we have this conversation again after Christmas?'

Ruby hated procrastinating but she could see that perhaps Sebastian wasn't sure what he wanted at the moment.

'I suppose so,' she said. 'But trust me when I say, Sebastian, that we *will* be having this conversation again. I need to know where my life is going.' *And when my heart is going to be broken,* came the suddenly depressing thought.

'And where do you want it to go, Ruby?' he asked, sitting back and watching her closely.

Ruby sat back also, the suspicion forming that he was trying to see if she wanted more from him than he was prepared to give. If she pressed him, he might end things here and now. If she wanted their relationship, such as it was, to continue, then she had to lighten things up.

She hoped her shrug looked nonchalant. 'Well, as I told you, I want to become a social worker. And to do that, I need a secure roof over my head and time to study. I suppose after Georgia gets back I'll try to get another job as a housekeeper here in Sydney. I don't really want to live with one of my brothers.'

'You still don't want to get married?'

'Lord no!' she exclaimed straight away. To say she wanted to marry him would be the kiss of death.

His sigh could have been relief. Or something else. Ruby wasn't sure and was afraid to hope.

'I'm sorry, Sebastian,' she said, and he threw her a questioning glance.

'Sorry about what?'

'It's Christmas, for heaven's sake. Time to be merry and have fun, not get all serious about the future. We'll worry about next year next year, okay?'

'Okay,' he said slowly, leaving Ruby with the impression that something was still bothering him.

'We should get going soon,' she suggested. 'The traffic is only going to get worse as the day wears on.'

The day ended well after that, their moods having lightened. They chatted away during the drive home, enjoyed dinner together that night, then went to bed together. Ruby wallowing in the pretence that they were, if not really married, then acting as if they were. And if there was a tiny little niggle still at the back of her mind, she steadfastly ignored it.

CHAPTER TWENTY-SEVEN

'HERE ARE THE books you asked for,' Sebastian said as he placed them on the tray table next to Zack's bed.

'Thanks,' Zack said, picking them up and reading the blurbs before looking up. 'I'll enjoy these. So tell me, Seb, how long have you been sleeping with Ruby?'

Sebastian wasn't surprised that Zack had twigged. After all, he already knew how much he fancied her.

'Since a week before the Christmas party,' Sebastian confessed.

Zack looked surprised. 'That long.'

'We decided to keep it a secret.'

'*We* decided to keep it a secret. Or *you* decided to keep it a secret.'

'I guess it was my idea. But Ruby didn't object.'

Zack made a tsking sound. 'I expected better of you than that. Ruby's a nice girl, as you went to great pains to tell me. She won't be happy with being your secret bit on the side for long. You must know that.'

'She doesn't want to get married,' Sebastian said with a sigh.

'What are you talking about? *You* don't want to get married, either. But marriage isn't the only card in the pack, Seb. You could ask her to be your girlfriend. What's wrong with that?'

'Nothing. I've actually already done that. And we won't be keeping our relationship a secret for much longer. We're letting the cat out of the bag on Christmas Day. But the strange thing is, Zack, I've realised I *do* want to get married. I thought I only wanted her to love me but I want more. I want her to be my wife.'

Zack's eyebrows almost hit the ceiling. 'Wow. Now you've really surprised me. You, Mr I-don't-ever-want-to-fall-in-love-and-get-married-again Marshall. Not that I'm surprised it's Ruby who's stolen your heart. She's a great girl. If you hadn't warned me off I might have fallen for her myself.'

'Didn't you hear what I said? She doesn't want to get married.'

'Did she say that to you?'

'Loud and clear.'

'Did you tell her you love her?'

'Well…no…'

'It might be an idea to tell her,' came his dry advice.

'She won't believe me.'

'Then it's up to you to convince her, isn't it? Pull out all stops. Go all romantic. I know you're not used to romantic gestures, buddy, but they work.'

Sebastian had to smile. 'You'd know. But you're undoubtedly right.'

'Of course I'm right. Faint heart never won fair lady.'

'No wonder you get the women, Zack. Poetry, no less. Now I have to get going. I have lots to do.' Already Sebastian's mind was buzzing with ideas. But they would take time. And effort. And money.

At least he had no shortage in that department.

'Good luck,' Zack called after him.

Luck, Sebastian decided as he hurried away, had little to do with success in life.

His first job after leaving the hospital was to go shopping. For a ring. Sebastian refused to countenance failure, so a ring was what he would need. Eventually. After what proved to be a long shopping expedition, he dropped in at the extremely popular Cafe Sydney and spent a small fortune, getting what he also wanted.

It was well after lunchtime as he drove away from the city, hunger pangs telling him he needed to eat. But he needed to get home more. He wanted to see his Ruby. Just *see* her. He didn't need to do anything else.

She wasn't at home, however, when he got there. He texted her immediately and found out she was at the supermarket, stocking up on food, plus a few last-minute gifts. She would be home soon.

Not soon enough for his stomach, Sebastian thought, so he made himself a sandwich and coffee.

'Didn't you eat in town?' she asked when she saw him.

'No,' he said between mouthfuls, his gaze drinking her in at the same time.

'Then what took you so long?'

He could hardly tell her the truth. *I was looking for the right ring for you, my darling.*

But he decided on a partial truth.

'After I visited Zack, I went shopping for something for you. For Christmas.'

'Really? That's sweet.'

'Unfortunately, I couldn't seem to decide what to buy. In the end I settled for taking you out somewhere special instead. I have a booking for lunch at Cafe Sydney on Christmas Eve.'

Her eyes lit up. 'But isn't that a pretty exclusive place?'

'Yes.'

'Then how did you manage to get a table this late? You said all the restaurants would be booked out.'

'I'm a regular customer there,' he said. 'They always keep a table or two free for regular patrons,' he lied. The truth was that he'd made them an offer they couldn't refuse. It would be the most expensive lunch he'd ever had. But it would be worth it. It already was, by the excited look on her face.

A happy Sebastian tucked into the rest of his sandwich whilst Ruby unpacked her shopping bags.

'Are you going to come with me to visit Zack tomorrow?' he asked her as he ate.

'No. Haven't you heard? The news about his attack is out. It was on the midday news.'

Sebastian swore, then sighed. 'I suppose it was too much to expect to keep it quiet for long.'

'Every man and his dog will be trying to interview him,' Ruby said.

Sebastian laughed. 'I don't like their chances. He won't even do media for the show. Its success comes mainly from word of mouth.'

'They'll still try. And all his work colleagues will be visiting. So no, I won't be going in with you. Sorry.'

'I'll have to go. Keep the vultures at bay.'

'I have things to do, anyway. Present wrapping mostly. I've organised to go over to see Liam and Oliver tomorrow night so we can catch up and exchange presents. Oh, golly,' she exclaimed. 'I just realised I forgot to buy wrapping paper, and gift tags. Truly, my head's not screwed on properly today. Janice said I was off with the pixies and she's right.'

Sebastian could only hope that might have something to do with him.

'Could you buy some wrapping paper for the presents I bought for Mum at the same time?' he asked.

'Yes, of course. I'll wrap them up as well.'

'You're a life-saver. What would I do without you?'

'You'd have Georgia,' she said dryly. 'Or Gloria. Or Janice.'

'Not the same as you,' he said warmly.

'Flatterer,' she said, but with a smile on her face. 'I think you've been spending too much time with Zack. His charm is beginning to wear off onto you.'

Sebastian tried not to feel offended. 'I'll have you know I can be charming when I want to be.'

She laughed. 'Perhaps I just wasn't there at the time.'

'Charm can be shallow,' he pointed out, quite seriously. 'Far better that a man be decent, and sincere.'

She stopped what she was doing and smiled at him. 'It's all right, Sebastian. You don't have to change for me. I like you just the way you are.'

CHAPTER TWENTY-EIGHT

CHRISTMAS EVE FINALLY CAME, the last few days having given Ruby some hope that her relationship with Sebastian might develop into something permanent. She didn't go so far as to imagine love and marriage yet, but who knew? Sebastian was certainly a different man nowadays compared to the rather rude individual she'd first met and who'd been determined not to have a woman in his life ever again after the death of his wife.

The man who took her to bed every night was not that man. Not even remotely.

She dressed carefully for her lunch with Sebastian. She didn't wear the red dress—that was reserved for Christmas Day—but another pretty dress she'd picked out recently, teamed with wedged sandals in a neutral colour. She left her hair down, her only jewellery a gold pendant her mother had given her for her sixteenth birthday. Her make-up was subtle, her perfume equally so.

Sebastian had gone to visit Zack as usual, catching the ferry in so he could have a drink at lunchtime and not be over the driving limit. She was catching a ferry too; the service from Mosman was very good. Ruby had never been to Cafe Sydney before but she knew it was on the top floor of the Customs building, just across from the quay, only a short walk from the ferry terminal.

Ruby did her best not to overreact to Sebastian's invitation but it was impossible not to feel both excited and, yes, positive. That he was taking her out in public was a big step. It was a proper date, not like the other day when they'd stopped off at some small coffee house in the city. Ruby had looked up Cafe Sydney on the Internet and it was one of *the* places to be seen in Sydney. The dining was superb, and so was the view of the bridge and the harbour.

Given its popularity with the rich and famous, they could easily run into people he knew. What would he say to them? she wondered. Would he introduce her as his housekeeper, or as his date?

Only time would tell, she supposed, her stomach aflutter with anticipation.

The weather was wonderful, neither too hot nor too windy. And not a sign of rain or the storms that often plagued Sydney at this time of year. Ruby stepped off the ferry right on twelve-thirty, which meant she would be a few minutes late, even later when the lights turned red, stopping her from crossing the road. As she waited, she sent Sebastian a text saying she was nearly there. He answered That's okay straight away, which brought a sigh of relief. The lights eventually turned green but Ruby still hurried across to the Customs building and there was another minute or two delay because the lifts were busy.

It was a slightly flustered Ruby who was shown to their table at a quarter to one.

Sebastian was already there, looking handsome and sinfully sexy in designer jeans and a blue top, the same colour as his eyes. He stood up when she arrived, like the gentleman he was, and gave her a sweet kiss on the cheek before telling the hovering waiter to give them a few minutes before ordering.

'Sorry, I'm late,' she said on sitting down. 'If I'd caught the previous ferry I would have been too early.'

'It's perfectly all right, Ruby. And may I say you were worth waiting for? You look utterly gorgeous.'

'Oh,' she said, even more flustered now. The way he was looking at her, if she didn't know better she might think he was in love with her. Only then did she glance away from his eyes at her surroundings, her heart beating like mad. 'Oh, my goodness, what a wonderful view,' she said. It looked even better in reality than in the photographs online, especially from their table, which was out on a balcony. 'And what a wonderful place. This is one of the best Christmas presents I've ever had. Thank you so much, Sebastian.'

'My pleasure,' he said, and poured her a glass of champagne from the bottle that he'd obviously already ordered.

'The trouble is, I feel extra guilty now about not buying you anything for Christmas.'

She had tried, but what did you buy a seriously rich man who already had everything he wanted? She didn't dare buy him clothes. Sebastian only wore designer brands, which were out of her reach, financially.

Buying presents for her brothers had been easy compared to Sebastian. He was just impossible!

'You don't have to buy me anything, you know,' he said.

'But I wanted to. And I tried. But I couldn't think of anything. Help me out here, Sebastian. Tell me something you want that I can afford.'

'You don't need to buy me anything, Ruby. You've already given me something incredibly valuable.'

'What's that?' she asked, perplexed.

'Happiness,' he said. 'You've made me truly happy again. Trust me when I say it's something I haven't been for a long time.'

'Oh,' she said, touched, but a little sad too.

'Before you came into my life, Ruby, the best I could say about myself was that I was busy. Busy and financially successful. I suppose I got some satisfaction from that. But it's not the same as having someone in your life to come home to, someone you care about.'

Ruby sucked in sharply. Caring was very close to love, but it wasn't quite the same. Was it possible he did love her but couldn't bring himself to say it? They weren't the easiest words to say. She hadn't said she loved him, either. She didn't want to risk spoiling what they had. Which was incredible. He really was a good man. And terribly intelligent. When they'd gone to bed together every night this week, they'd talked endlessly about a wide range of topics before going to sleep. He seemed to know something about everything. He'd travelled all over the world, whereas she had only been to New Zealand. Not that he ever made her feel inferior. He wasn't like that.

'Have I said something I shouldn't?' he asked when she didn't continue with their conversation, her mind having gone off on a tangent.

'No, not at all. I'm happy that I've made you happy.'

He tipped his head to one side as he regarded her closely. 'But have I made you happy, Ruby?'

'Happy?' she repeated, not sure if she would describe herself as truly happy.

She wished…

A wry smile lifted the corner of her mouth. She wished for too much. That was the truth of the matter.

'You make me very happy in bed,' she said somewhat flippantly.

Her answer didn't seem to please him. He frowned for a long moment. It wasn't until he smiled that she finally relaxed.

Ruby picked up her glass of champagne and lifted it in a toast. 'To being happy,' she said, and clinked her glass against his.

'Indeed,' he returned.

A man suddenly appeared by their table, a well-dressed portly fellow of around sixty who had money written all over him. 'What are you toasting, Sebastian?' he asked. 'And who is this lovely lady you're with?'

Ruby immediately tensed, waiting to hear Sebastian's answer.

'Trust you to come sniffing around, Gregory, when you see a new beauty on the scene. But no, Ruby's not an actor. And not for poaching in any way. She's my girlfriend. My *live-in* girlfriend,' he emphasised. 'Ruby, this is Gregory Bardon, who runs Bardon's casting agency. He's always on the lookout for new talent. Gregory, this is Ruby.'

'Ruby,' the man repeated, taking her hand and lifting it to his lips in an old-fashioned kiss. 'Charmed. You are a lucky dog, Sebastian. Live-in, did you say?'

'I did.'

'Amazing. And there I was, all these years, thinking you might be gay.'

'Really? Whatever gave you that idea?'

'Just a rumour I heard once. Clearly I was wrong. Lovely to have met you, Ruby. Happy Christmas.'

'Same to you too,' Ruby called after him, struggling not to laugh.

'You should see the look on your face,' she said to Sebastian when they were alone again.

He finally saw the funny side and laughed as well.

They had a lovely lunch together, the champagne gorgeous, the food divine, and the trip home on the ferry a lot better than driving. Christmas Eve traffic was always a nightmare. Ruby was glad she'd taken her brothers' presents over to them the night before. They'd had an enjoyable evening together, Oliver coming over to Liam's place so they could exchange gifts. They'd opened them then and there, Ruby wanting the pleasure of giving hers in person. She'd bought her brothers and their partners a very stylish vase each to go with the expensive sheets and towels. The girls had loved everything. Ruby had been just as happy with her own gifts. Now she wouldn't run out of perfume for ages, and she had lots of lovely books to read.

By the time she and Sebastian arrived home, the

afternoon had warmed up and Sebastian suggested they have a swim.

'Good idea,' Ruby said.

'You can even wear that dastardly bikini if you like.'

Ruby raised her eyebrows at him. 'Are you sure about that? You might not be able to control yourself.'

'I can always control myself when I know there are better things to come. I'm looking forward to taking you to bed tonight and making love to you for hours.'

Ruby's heart flipped over at his words. Had he really said making love, instead of having sex? Did he mean it or was it just a slip of the tongue?

'Don't you mean have sex for hours?' she couldn't help saying.

'No,' he said, his eyes very serious on her. 'I meant exactly what I said. I want to make love to you, Ruby, because I'm in love with you.'

Ruby decided later that she must have looked like a goldfish with her mouth hanging open and her eyes wide with shock.

'You're in love with me?' she said at last after she'd drawn in several scoops of much-needed air.

'Madly,' he said, smiling as he pulled her into his arms.

'Oh, Lord.'

His smile suddenly faded to a less confident expression. 'Is that good news or bad news?'

She blinked, stunned that he would think him loving her was bad news. But then she recalled the things she'd said to him in the past. She'd actually called him a bastard on one occasion. She'd also said she didn't

particularly like him. It was no wonder he was looking a little worried. Even today at the lunch, she'd only
said he made her happy in bed, reducing their relationship to little more than sex.

'It's good news,' she said tenderly. 'Very good news.
Because I'm madly in love with you too.'

Now it was his mouth's turn to gape open. 'You
are? You really are?'

'I really am.'

He beamed down at her like a child on Christmas
morning. 'You've no idea how glad I am to hear that.
I thought… No, it doesn't matter what I thought. All
that matters is that we love each other.'

'Madly,' she added.

'Yes, madly. But also deeply. It's not just lust talking here, Ruby. I really, really love you. *You*, the beautiful, sweet, wonderful person that you are.'

Tears pricked at her eyes. 'I never thought a man
would ever love me like that,' she choked out. 'Oh,
Sebastian, you've made me so happy.'

'*I've* made *you* happy? You've put me on cloud
nine, Ruby, and I don't think I'll ever come down.'
He hugged her close, Ruby laying her head against his
chest. His heart was thumping behind his ribs, and so
was hers. She stayed in the warmth of his embrace for
a while before lifting her face to his.

'Could we perhaps skip the swim and just go to
bed?' she suggested softly.

Sebastian could not believe the feelings that coursed
through him as he lay in bed with Ruby snuggled up
next to him. He'd loved Jennifer but what he felt for

Ruby seemed so much stronger. It was a for-ever kind of love, with the strength to face whatever problems life would throw at them as a couple.

It was time, he realised, to take the next step. Maybe it was a little premature but, as Zack said, faint heart never won fair lady.

'Ruby?' he murmured, giving her shoulder a little shake.

'Hmmm?'

'Are you awake?'

She sighed as she rolled onto her back and looked at him. 'I am now.'

'I was going to wait but I can't. I have to ask you now.'

'Ask me what?'

'Will you marry me?'

She sat bolt upright in the bed, the sheet falling off her naked body. She snatched it back up over her breasts, her eyes wide with shock. Sebastian felt his heart sink.

'You don't mean that,' she said. 'You can't. I mean…'

'I do mean it,' he insisted. 'I told you you'd made me break all those rules I was living my life by. They were stupid rules, Ruby. Cowardly rules. Yes, I was devastated when Jennifer died but I think I was more devastated by the way she handled it, pushing me away, not letting me help nurse her. You would never be like that. We'd handle anything life throws at us together. Fight it together.'

By now tears were streaming down Ruby's cheeks.

'That's beautiful, Sebastian,' she choked out. 'And yes, I will marry you. Wherever and whenever you want.'

The joy that exploded in Sebastian's heart was almost impossible for him to describe.

'In that case, as soon as possible, please,' he said, kissing the tears from her face. 'Unless, of course, you want a big fancy wedding.'

'Lord, no. Though I do want a proper bridal gown, and lots and lots of photos. We can have the ceremony here, in the garden.'

'Sounds marvellous. I'll ask Zack to be best man.'

'And my brothers can give me away.'

'Done! Now I just have to go and get something,' he said, scrambling out of the bed and heading into his walk-in wardrobe. Ruby's heart leapt when he returned with a very small bag, one from a jewellery shop.

Surely not, she thought.

'It took me ages to find the right one,' he said as he produced the ring box and sank down on his knees by the bed, still stark naked.

When he flipped the box open, Ruby stared down at the most beautiful ring she'd ever seen. In the middle of a rose-gold setting was a huge ruby, encircled by diamonds. Quite big diamonds. It must have cost a fortune!

'A perfect ruby for my perfect Ruby,' Sebastian said as he lifted it out and slipped it on her engagement-ring finger.

'Oh, Sebastian, it's stunning. And it fits perfectly. How did you manage that?'

'A combination of luck, my powers of observation

and a very experienced jeweller. You really like it, then?'

'I adore it. But, Sebastian, I can't possibly wear it yet. And certainly not tomorrow at your sister's place. Your family will really think things about me now.'

'What kind of things?' he asked as he climbed into bed next to her.

'Well, you know. Like I'm some kind of scheming gold-digger.'

He laughed. '*You?* A gold-digger? Now that's a funny one.'

'I'm serious. After all, we've only known each other a few weeks.'

'Has it really only been that long? It feels like an eternity.'

'I know what you mean. I feel the same way.'

'Trust me when I say my family won't think any such things about you, Ruby darling,' he said as he kissed her tenderly on her forehead, her nose, her cheek. 'My mother will be especially delighted. Now, no more doubts. You will wear your engagement ring tomorrow and that's that.'

'Goodness, you can be forceful when you want to be, Mr Marshall.'

'I can. And you are to call both your brothers tomorrow and let them know as well.'

'They are going to be seriously surprised. I told them I was never getting married.'

'It's a woman's privilege to change her mind.'

'And a man's,' she pointed out.

'True. Now can we stop with the chit-chat and celebrate our engagement as lovers should?'

CHAPTER TWENTY-NINE

'Wow!' Sebastian exclaimed. 'That is one gorgeous dress.'

Ruby preened. 'Someone with taste chose it for me.'

'Someone who knew it would suit you too, especially the colour.'

'It doesn't look too sexy, does it?' she asked, suddenly swamped by her worries over his family's reaction to their engagement.

Sebastian scowled. 'Don't be nervous. You have nothing to worry about.'

Ruby sighed. 'I can't help worrying a bit.'

'Then we'd better get going so we can get the surprise of our engagement over and done with and you can stop worrying.'

'My mother used to call it the heebie-jeebies,' she told him.

He smiled. 'What a wonderful expression. I like the sound of your mother.'

Ruby swallowed. 'She would have liked you too. She liked manly men. She thought Gregory Peck was gorgeous, and you know what? You look a bit like him.'

'I'll take that as a compliment. But I would prefer to

be compared with someone a little more current. Are you ready? How do *I* look? Not too casual?'

He was wearing dark blue shorts, a red and navy striped T-shirt and navy loafers.

'You look great,' she complimented. 'And look, we're colour-coordinated. That red in your T-shirt is the same red as my dress.'

'You're right. We do look good together. Come on. No, wait! Have you rung your brothers?'

Ruby's heart skipped a beat. 'Er...no. I'll do that later, when they're together at the restaurant. That way I only have to make the one call.'

'Good thinking. Okay, let's go.'

Ruby's nerves returned during the relatively short drive to Gloria's. They didn't have to pick up Frieda on the way, as she'd stayed the night before at her daughter's place. When they pulled up outside a house, which Ruby presumed was Gloria's, she sucked in a couple of deep breaths and told herself not to be so silly.

The house, Ruby noted, was rather old. One of those federation homes with dark verandas and stained-glass windows. It was in good condition, however, the front door freshly painted in very fashionable black. The garden was traditional, with lots of rose bushes and hedges.

Two teenage boys burst out of the house before Sebastian and Ruby could get out of the car. They looked about fourteen and sixteen, both with dark hair and blue eyes, like their uncle, confirming Ruby's suspicion that Gloria's blonde hair might not be natural.

'Hi, Unc,' the older one said. 'Happy Christmas.

So this is Ruby. Hi, Ruby. Mum was right, Alex. She said the new housekeeper was a looker.'

'Matthew Chambers,' Sebastian said. 'Stop being cheeky.'

'Ruby, this is Matthew and Alexander. My nephews.'

Both boys pulled faces at the use of their full names.

'And this,' he said as he put a loving arm around Ruby, 'is not just my housekeeper. She's your soon-to-be Auntie Ruby.'

The boys were goggle-eyed for a moment, then they dashed inside, yelling out as they went.

'Uncle Sebastian's got engaged,' both of them chorused loudly.

'That's put a cat among the pigeons,' Sebastian muttered as everyone else emerged onto the front veranda, their faces mirroring shock but not displeasure. In fact, when they saw it was Ruby with Sebastian they all looked heartily relieved. Gloria rushed out to the car, grabbing Ruby's left hand and staring down at the ring.

'Oh, my God!' she exclaimed. 'It's true. Wow, this is fantastic.'

Frieda joined them as well, beaming broadly. 'You finally saw sense, Sebastian.'

'Yes, Mum.'

'Welcome to our family, Ruby. I couldn't be more pleased.' And she gave Ruby a hug.

'Thank you, Frieda.'

'Ruby was a bit worried that you might think this all happened a little fast,' Sebastian said.

'Don't be ridiculous,' Frieda replied. 'You're both old enough to know your own minds. When are you getting married? Soon, I hope. I'm not getting any younger, either.'

Sebastian smiled at her. 'We thought in about six weeks. It takes a month to get the licence. Ruby wants to have the ceremony at home, in the garden.'

'Excellent idea,' Gloria jumped in. 'Now, I have to get back to the dinner. Matthew and Alexander, help your uncle bring in the presents. And, Henry,' she directed at the man behind them, who Ruby presumed was her husband, 'take the happy couple inside and get them a drink. We have lots of celebrating to do today.'

And celebrate they did, all Ruby's qualms put to rest by the warmth of her welcome into the family.

Dinner was a very traditional turkey, which was cooked to perfection. Dessert was also traditional—plum pudding and custard. Ruby loved it all because it reminded her of the Christmases they'd had when her mother was alive. It wasn't until they were enjoying coffee and Christmas cake out on the back veranda afterwards that Sebastian reminded her to ring her brothers.

She groaned. 'Do I have to do it today?'

'Yes,' came his firm reply.

Ruby sighed, made her excuses and went inside to where she'd left her handbag on the hall stand. It was with great reluctance that she drew out her phone and brought up Liam's number, her stomach in knots at the thought of how they would react to her news.

'Sis!' he answered straight away. 'We were just talking about you. Merry Christmas, by the way.'

'Same to you,' she said. 'Are you still at the restaurant?'

'Yes. Just. Why?'

'I have something to tell you and Oliver. And the girls too, of course.'

'Sounds serious. I'll put my phone on speaker so that they can all hear.'

'Oh. All right.'

'Out with it. What have you done, sis? Nothing drastic, I hope.'

'Not drastic. No. A bit surprising, though.'

She heard whispering in the background.

'Okay,' Oliver joined in. 'What is it?' Oliver was the more forceful of the twins.

Ruby took a deep breath first. 'Sebastian and I, we…well, we're going to get married.'

Ruby heard various gasps.

'You're not joking, are you?' Oliver said.

'No.'

'Do you love him?' Oliver asked.

'I do. Very much so.'

'He's a lucky man.'

'Does he love you?' Liam piped up.

'He does,' Ruby said without hesitation. 'Madly, he says.'

'Oh, how romantic!' Rachel and Lara exclaimed at exactly the same time. Maybe they were catching that habit from the twins, who often said exactly the same thing at the same time.

'When's the wedding?' Liam and Oliver asked in unison.

Ruby smiled. 'Soon.'

'It's not a shotgun wedding, is it?' Oliver demanded to know.

Ruby laughed. 'No, Oliver, it's not.'

'Just thought I should ask. In that case, congrats, sis. As long as you're happy, we're happy.'

'I'm very happy.'

'Yes, we can hear it in your voice.'

They talked on for a little while until Ruby said she had to get back to the others. When she returned to the back veranda, everyone looked at her expectantly.

'All right?' Sebastian asked. 'They were supportive, I hope.'

'Very. They were delighted that I asked them both to give me away on the day.'

'I rang Zack at the hospital whilst you were speaking to your brothers,' Sebastian said. 'Told him the good news. He was thrilled to pieces. Agreed to be best man as well. So that's all done. Now we can settle back and enjoy the rest of Christmas Day.'

It was a grand day full of fun and festivities, the best Christmas either Ruby or Sebastian had had for a long time. But it would not be the last great Christmas, Ruby vowed when it came time to leave.

'Next year,' she told everyone at the door, 'Christmas will be at our house.' And she privately promised herself that there would be a huge tree and lots and lots of lights, even over the front of the house.

CHAPTER THIRTY

Their wedding day, six weeks later...

RUBY SPUN ROUND at the loud knocking on her bed-room door.

'Are you ready yet, Ruby?' Oliver called out. 'It's time.'

Time...

Time to get married. Time to face the kind of future Ruby had never imagined for herself. But falling in love for real made you change your mind about things. Her vow never to trust a man with her happiness had dissipated under the obvious sincerity of Sebastian's love. For he had had to make massive changes, too. Ruby sometimes thought of his first wife, but she wasn't jealous of her, or Sebastian's long-ago love for her. Ruby suspected Jennifer had been an emotionally damaged person, not capable of giving true love in return. She'd hurt Sebastian terribly when she'd pushed him away during her final days, a hurt that had taken years to heal.

But he was all healed now, Ruby thought happily as she hurried over to open the bedroom door.

'Wow, sis,' both her brothers said as one.

'I do look a bit wow, don't I?' She preened, doing a complete turn so they could look at the back of her dress—and her hair—as well as the front.

Her white bridal gown was strapless, with a beaded bodice, a cinched-in waist and a very low back. The skirt was a full-length fall of shimmering silk that skimmed the floor. Ruby had decided against a veil, and instead pulled her hair back and braided it in a loose plait down her back, a circlet of flowers on her head. The only jewellery she was wearing besides her engagement ring were the ruby and diamond earrings Sebastian had presented her with over breakfast and which had brought her to tears.

Ruby was aware the dress was a little tighter now than at the first fitting—the result of her being pregnant. Not that she intended telling her brothers that little piece of news. They'd accuse her of having a shotgun wedding again. Sebastian knew, of course. But then it had been *his* idea to let nature take its course when she'd forgotten to take her pill on Christmas Day. Both of them had been thrilled when the test had come up positive a fortnight ago, which just showed how far they'd come. They were already planning names. Ava for a girl—named after her mother—and Jack for a boy—named after Sebastian's father.

'Come on,' Oliver urged. 'The celebrant is getting antsy.'

'Don't you mean Sebastian?' Liam said laughingly.

Ruby smoothed her dress before reaching for her bouquet of red and white roses. 'Let's go.'

Once outside the bedroom and in the roomier hallway, Liam and Oliver linked arms with her, and led her out to where the wedding was to take place.

Ruby had decided on a simple ceremony on the back lawn, to be moved inside if it rained. But the day was fine and clear, and not too hot or humid. She'd been blessed with the weather because February in Sydney was often stifling. As it was, the wedding guests would not be uncomfortable today, sitting outside on the white plastic chairs that had been set up in rows in front of a portable wooden stage with an artificial rose arbour decorating it and the obligatory strip of red carpet leading up to it.

Ruby had insisted on the Christmas lights being left up. The ceremony was scheduled for six o'clock and instead of a fancy sit-down meal for guests, she'd booked the same caterers and DJ they'd had for the Christmas party. The guest list was pretty much the same as well, with a few family extras.

Ruby's heart swelled as she noted there wasn't an empty chair, everyone clearly having turned up. They all had their phones out, snapping photographs. She wanted lots of photos. But not ones taken by an official photographer, just lots of informal happy snaps. Her heart swelled further when she saw Sebastian standing at the end of the red carpet, a huge smile breaking over his handsome face when he saw her. And possibly relief that she'd shown up at last.

All the men in her bridal party were wearing black tuxedos, with red roses in their lapels, matching the red roses in her bouquet. Ruby knew they would look fabulous in their wedding photos, for which she'd already bought frames. Sebastian had been aghast at their number, then had laughed. He knew when he was beaten.

Ruby made her way down the aisle, smiling left and right as she went. She beamed at Georgia, who'd flown up for the wedding but was going back to Melbourne afterwards. For good.

'It's no use,' she'd told Ruby and Sebastian over the phone. 'I won't be coming back at all. I can't live without those kids. I'd miss them too much.' She'd moved in with her sister and taken a job at a nearby hotel where she only worked part-time.

Ruby didn't mind at all. She didn't want a housekeeper. She had Janice and Tom, and that would be enough. When Sebastian had suggested a nanny for after the baby was born, she'd almost choked on the spot. A nanny? No way.

Speaking of Janice and Tom, there they were, grinning at her. She grinned right back, secretly thinking that she should have had the DJ play 'Dancing Queen' at that moment, just like in the movie *Muriel's Wedding*. But perhaps not. Sebastian's family might not be amused.

Ruby moved further down the red carpet, bestowing smiles on all of Sebastian's work colleagues, but reserving her biggest smile for his immediate family, who were now *her* family. There were Gloria and Henry and their boys, sitting alongside Frieda, all looking resplendent. Finally, she looked back at the man she was about to marry, who was standing there impatiently, with his much more patient best friend by his side. Zack winked at her.

What a naughty man he was! Very naughty, according to nurse Susan, who'd shocked everyone by moving into his penthouse with him when he left hospital. Zack pretended he'd hired her as his private nurse, but Ruby had always suspected differently. And she'd been right. Susan was here somewhere in the crowd of guests. Ruby winked back at Zack before shifting her gaze back to Sebastian. What was he thinking at this moment? she wondered.

What a cheeky minx she was, Sebastian thought when he saw Ruby wink at Zack. But a sheer delight in every way. He loved everything about her, especially her down-to-earth nature and her lack of interest in becoming a socialite. She could have had a huge wedding, in a cathedral no less, with a custom-made designer dress, half a dozen bridesmaids and the reception held at some swanky function centre. Instead, she'd insisted on this simple ceremony, with a dress bought off the rack, a cake made by the local bakery, no bridesmaids, and a casual party afterwards with nibbles and finger food. The only thing he'd had a say in was the champagne, and he'd insisted on the very best from France. He'd also put his foot down where the honeymoon was concerned and booked a five-star luxury apartment on Hamilton Island for two weeks. He would have liked to take Ruby away for longer but Harvest Productions was back in full swing and he really needed to be hands-on, especially where *Battle at the Bar* was concerned. The writers of that show could occasionally go off on a dangerous tangent without a close eye being kept on them.

Thinking of close eyes brought Sebastian's gaze

back to Ruby. Lord, but she had one lush figure, even more so now that she was expecting. A smile spread across his face at the thought that they were going to have a child together. It was an amazing thought, really, considering that before he met Ruby he hadn't even wanted to get married again. She'd changed him, that was for sure. For the better, according to Zack. Then again, she'd changed Zack too, made him see that he too could commit to one woman and be happy. Apparently, he and Susan were very serious about each other, which pleased Sebastian no end. Zack deserved to be happy.

'You're looking very pleased with yourself,' Ruby whispered after her brothers had unhanded her and returned to their seats.

'I am. I was just thinking what a lucky man I am to be marrying a girl as gorgeous as you. By the way, I love that dress.'

Ruby smiled. 'Oliver and Liam said you'd like it.'

He grinned at her. 'Did they now?'

The celebrant clearing his throat brought them back to the present moment.

'Shall we begin?' he asked quietly.

'Fire away,' Ruby said, loud enough for some of the guests to hear, since they laughed.

It was a happy ceremony. And a quick one. Zack produced the rings on cue and all was over within minutes, and Sebastian kissed her enthusiastically and passionately. Everyone stood up and clapped, with more photos being taken than at Sydney's opening ceremony.

Guests said afterwards it was the best wedding they'd ever been to.

* * *

Ava Frieda Marshall made her entrance into the world by Caesarean section three weeks early, weighing just over two kilos. Despite being small, she was extremely healthy. Jack Henry Marshall followed his sister by only a minute. He was a more robust three kilos, screaming his head off and making his presence known as only boys could. Sebastian and Ruby had known they were expecting twins but they could not have anticipated, however, the rush of love that overwhelmed them both at the actual arrival of their son and daughter. Sebastian cried as he videoed everything, Ruby in tears herself. Frieda blubbered away on a chair in the corner, having almost fainted at one stage. But she recovered quickly when Sebastian put Ava into her arms.

'Oh, what a precious little darling she is.'

Ruby never relented on hiring a nanny but Frieda came to stay for the first couple of months. And she was a great help. After that, Frieda came often. Jack, surprisingly, developed into a cruisy baby, despite his noisy arrival at the hospital. Ava fretted a little with colic for the first few weeks and often would not settle until her father came home to rock her to sleep in his arms. Zack and Susan were godparents at their christening, stunning Sebastian and Ruby when they announced they were expecting a little bundle of their own. They married just before their daughter Delvine, named after Zack's mother, was born. Naturally, Sebastian and Ruby were her godparents. In the years to come, the four adults and three children would often go on holidays together.

Battle at the Bar went on to be the most successful show on Australian TV for a decade, watched all over the world. It was also the winner of many awards, which Ruby displayed around the house along with a plethora of family photos. Ruby eventually achieved her ambition to get a degree in social science, working part-time as a high-school counsellor after her own precious twins started school.

The principal said she was the best counsellor they'd ever had.

* * * * *

*If you were head over heels for
The Billionaire's Cinderella Housekeeper,
then you'll adore these other stories by
Miranda Lee!*

The Magnate's Tempestuous Marriage
The Tycoon's Outrageous Proposal
The Tycoon's Scandalous Proposition
The Italian's Unexpected Love-Child
Maid for the Untamed Billionaire

All available now!

#3897 THE SECRET THAT CAN'T BE HIDDEN
Rich, Ruthless & Greek
by Caitlin Crews

Kendra Connolly has never forgotten her fleeting first encounter with billionaire Balthazar Skalas. When they're reunited, she gives in to temptation—completely. It's a decision made in the heat of the moment that will change her life forever...

#3898 CINDERELLA IN THE BOSS'S PALAZZO
by Julia James

Haunted by his past, wealthy Italian Evandro has sworn off romance—but he can't ignore the chemistry with his daughter's fiery new tutor, Jenna. The pair may clash, but their attraction is ready to hit boiling point...

#3899 THE GREEK WEDDING SHE NEVER HAD
Innocent Summer Brides
by Chantelle Shaw

Eleanor broke off her engagement to devastatingly handsome tycoon Jace, believing he only wanted her family's business. Now to save it, she must accept his second proposal! And shockingly, their chemistry has lost none of its heat...

#3900 WAYS TO RUIN A ROYAL REPUTATION
Signed, Sealed...Seduced
by Dani Collins

King Luca never craved the throne, but to abdicate, he must become a royal disgrace! He'll need Amy Miller's PR genius to fan the flames of scandal, but passionate flames may just ignite in the process...

#3901 BRIDE BEHIND THE DESERT VEIL
The Marchetti Dynasty
by Abby Green
After surrendering to passion with a mystery woman, Sharif Marchetti must erase their desert encounter from his memory. Until they meet again...as he lifts the veil of his convenient wife!

#3902 THE ITALIAN'S FORBIDDEN VIRGIN
Those Notorious Romanos
by Carol Marinelli
Italian tycoon Gian de Luca knows Ariana Romano is off-limits. She's his mentor's daughter, and her drama queen reputation precedes her. But when he offers her comfort one night, he's shocked to discover she's a virgin. Perhaps he's been wrong about her all along...

#3903 HIS STOLEN INNOCENT'S VOW
The Queen's Guard
by Marcella Bell
For billionaire Drake Andros, only marriage and an heir from Helene d'Tierrza will recover what was stolen from him. Their chemistry may persuade her to help him, but her vow of innocence may complicate his plan...

#3904 ONE HOT NEW YORK NIGHT
Wanted: A Billionaire
by Melanie Milburne
A sizzling night of passion is exactly what Zoey Brackenfield needs. And since it's with Finn O'Connell, business rival and notorious playboy, there's zero chance of heartbreak. That is, until she starts craving his exhilarating touch...

YOU CAN FIND MORE INFORMATION ON UPCOMING HARLEQUIN TITLES, FREE EXCERPTS AND MORE AT HARLEQUIN.COM.

HPCNMRB0321

SPECIAL EXCERPT FROM

⊕ HARLEQUIN
PRESENTS

*For billionaire Drake Andros, only marriage and
an heir from Helene d'Tierrza will recover what
was stolen from him. Their chemistry may persuade
her to help him, but her vow of innocence may
complicate his plan...*

*Read on for a sneak preview of
Marcella Bell's next story for Harlequin Presents*
His Stolen Innocent's Vow.

"I can't," she repeated, her voice low and earnest. "I can't, because
when I went to him as he lay dying, I looked him in his eyes and
swore to him that the d'Tierrza line would end with me, that there
would be no d'Tierrza children to inherit the lands or title and
that I would see to it that the family name was wiped from the
face of the earth so that everything he had ever worked for, or
cared about, was lost to history, the legacy he cared so much about
nothing but dust. I swore to him that I would never marry and
never have children, that not a trace of his legacy would be left
on this planet."

For a moment, there was a pause, as if the room itself had
sucked in a hiss of irritation. The muscles in his neck tensed, then
flexed, though he remained otherwise motionless. He blinked as if
in slow motion, the movement a sigh, carrying something much
deeper than frustration, though no sound came out. Hel's chest
squeezed as she merely observed him. She felt like she'd let him
down in some monumental way, though they'd only just become
reacquainted. She struggled to understand why the sensation was
so familiar until she recognized the experience of being in the
presence of her father.

Then he opened his eyes again, and instead of the cold green disdain her heart expected, they still burned that fascinating warm brown—a heat that was a steady home fire, as comforting as the imaginary family she'd dreamed up as a child—and all of the taut disappointment in the air was gone.

Her vow was a hiccup in his plans. That he had a low tolerance for hiccups was becoming clear. How she knew any of this when he had revealed so little in his reaction, and her mind only now offered up hazy memories of him as a young man, she didn't know.

She offered a shrug and an airy laugh in consolation, mildly embarrassed about the whole thing though she was simultaneously unsure as to exactly why. "Otherwise, you know, I'd be all in. Despite the whole abduction…" Her cheeks were hot, likely bright pink, but it couldn't be helped, so she made the joke anyway, despite the risk that it might bring his eyes to her face, that it might mean their gazes locked again and he stole her breath again.

Of course, that was what happened. And then there was that smile again, the one that said he knew all about the strange, mesmerizing power he had over her, and it pleased him.

Whether he was the kind of man who used his power for good or evil had yet to be determined.

Either way, beneath that infuriating smile, deep in his endless brown eyes, was the sharp attunement of a predator locked on its target. "Give me a week." His face may not have changed, but his voice gave him away, a trace of hoarseness, as if his sails had been slashed and the wind slipped through them, threaded it, a strange hint of something Hel might have described as desperation…if it had come from anyone other than him.

"What?" she asked.

"Give me a week to change your mind."